Spomenka Štimec

CROA-TIAN WAR NOC- TURNAL

Translated from the Esperanto
by Sebastian Schulman

FAREWELL TO BELGRADE

My aunt had wanted to study journalism, something that was only possible in the capital. So, her parents got her ready for the great journey. It was 1948, just after the war, when life still ran on ration cards and nothing could be bought in the stores. They stitched together clothes for her from a good-looking piece of fabric taken from the bed. Grandmother gave her a large ring with an oval gemstone that the women in our family wore on their index fingers. Somehow it had survived the war. She also gave her a gold star-shaped necklace engraved with the message *this star is your happiness*. Both the star and her happiness would be stolen a few years later from underneath her pillow while she was out working with the labor brigades.

Five years later, my aunt came back home with a diploma and with a husband. Jobs had been promised to all the students, but in her last year, there was a sudden change—too many students had shifted their loyalties to the politician Milovan Đjilas and the school was closed. Students in their last year were allowed to graduate, but no one was given their promised employment.

Her husband had to serve in the army. She got a job in the village office, waiting for the arrival of their first child. They called the girl Sanja—*dream*. This was a time of many dreams. Was it really necessary to say that the new father was a Serb? "My husband is from Gospić," she probably said. The name said everything else.

A short time later, someone sent them word that a job was available in Belgrade. Again, they packed up their boxes. Sanja was sent to her grandmother's house in Lika, where she was raised until she was ready to go to school. Her brother, born a few years later, would be brought up in the same way. In the capital, my aunt's career as a journalist pushed life forward at a relentless pace.

At the age of six, Sanja moved to the capital to start school, timidly asking her new friends:

"Are there wolves here?"

"No wolves. Just criminals."

In the harsh region where she had lived, wolves were a great danger. In the capital, however, other dangers threatened.

Sanja and I each had only one grandfather. My other grandfather had died in Australia. I never knew him. Her other grandfather died in the pits of Jadovno. In Croatian, *jad* means pain, woe, sorrow. The same in Serbian. He was arrested during the Second World War. Every day his son would bring his pot of rations to the prison, until one day there was no one to pass the pot to. The corpses of the condemned were thrown into the pits of Jadovno and covered with lime.

Wrapped in a heavy blanket and hiding under the table, I listened to all the details of his disappearance.

"Why did he die?" I wondered aloud.

"Go play in the other room. This is not for children!"

If I had just been able to keep my mouth shut, I would know more. Thrown out of the circle of secrets, I never did get the full explanation. Later I understood—he was murdered by the Ustaše because he was a Serb, under the Independent State of Croatia.

According to our family's unwritten rule, the children from Croatia and Serbia were supposed to spend the greater part of their holidays together. We loved this rule—the smallest among us were always asking if we really had to wait one hundred sleeps until the cousins came back. Back then, one hundred seemed close to infinity.

Today I realize that our relatives did this on purpose, to cultivate in us the feeling that we would actually enjoy each other's company.

Our cousins from Belgrade were the most well-off. Living in the big city, they had everything at their disposal from an early age, things their parents gave them to unburden themselves from the guilt of spending too much time away from their kids.

Every summer at the end of June, the Belgrade cousins would come just as the black currants were ripening in the garden. From this great mass of berries, Grandmother would make fresh jam. It was warm outside—we wore knee socks. The kids carved out a special path between the currant bushes, which we jokingly called "The Avenue of Brotherhood and Unity," after the great highway of the same name that connected Zagreb and Belgrade. *Bratstvo i jedinstvo!* This was one of the most important slogans upon which socialist Yugoslavia stood—we were all brothers, striving for unity. So, we christened the currant allée with the concept of local socialist fraternity (only later did the fruit bushes acquire the added designation of an international "circle of harmony," taking a line from the Esperanto anthem—a further expansion of our view of the world). Somehow, it seemed that the biggest, juiciest bunches of currants grew out of the bounds of Brotherhood and Unity and so we took over the garden's other paths as well.

Those of us from Croatia rarely went to Belgrade. Too expensive. But how we relished the trip when the opportunity came. My aunt would take her niece by the hand and show her the city. That little hand belonged to me. The neighborhood was called *Zeleni Venac*—the "green wreath." Charming, no? I had grown up in Varaždin, a town with a renowned cemetery, always full of burial wreaths. Suddenly, my aunt dropped my clammy little hand. The main street. A green light. "Go!" She started to cross. But not me. I was afraid of cars. There were too many of them. She ran back, gave me her hand, and explained that the cars had to stop since their light was red. But I didn't believe that they would stop. They were going too fast! I might have been a naïve little village girl, but I had already learned not to trust anything.

My favorite thing in their Belgrade apartment was the rug. "When I grow up, I'm going to buy one just like it!" I whispered a secret promise to myself, staring at its expanse of green. I still haven't grown up quite enough to afford one. The rug was handmade, elegant. I had spent my youth on discount rags, factory mistakes bought cheaply, but in this carpet I discovered art. It was dark green, surrounded by tangles of branches where white birds made their homes. At its edge, you could read the artist's name woven into the fabric: *VUJAKLIJA*. Later, my love for Vujaklija grew by yet another small measure. His first name was Lazar. Just like Zamenhof, the creator of our language.

On one trip to the capital, my little brother got sick, having too eagerly devoured those Belgrade specialties, *pita zeljanica* and *pita od mesa*, and vomited all over the fabled rug. They used all sorts of brooms and brushes, bleach and other things to remove the stain while we put my brother to bed. If that had happened today, someone would have undoubtedly come up with a spiteful little couplet: *Croatian heave on Serbian weave!* But for me, Vujaklija's tapestry has remained among my most treasured memories. I have carried it with me my entire life and it has grown older with me, totally un- blemished.

There were a lot of things on that rug from Grandmother's house back in Croatia. Back then, I would stand before them in my grandmother's master bedroom, a piece of cloth in hand and the tedium of dusting ahead. How I hated to touch these delicate things. Besides, they looked so much prettier when it was some other cousin's turn to dust.

There was the rose-colored lamp with a stylized portrait of a young woman. All the way from the 19th century. Did someone bring it back from Vienna? The lamp stood in front of a mirror, making it seem as though the room had two such rose-colored fixtures. A small wheel on the side clicked and brought the bulb to light, although we never turned it on. Two long peacock feathers used to stick out of the top. By the time, my aunt got permission to take the lamp with her to Belgrade, the feathers had already disappeared. To come to

Belgrade and see the lamp again was like getting reacquainted with a younger version of myself. The lady of the lamp never grew old. She lived enveloped in romance and we were all in love with her.

Sanja once told me about an earthquake in Belgrade, how she grabbed the lamp and ran out to the elevator. Just picture it: "Quick! To the elevator with the rose-colored lamp!" we joked. Couldn't she have thought to take cover under something a bit sturdier?

With love and nostalgia, I often think about our family lamp. When I overhear those ugly tirades on the tram saying that we should bomb Belgrade to stop the war, I see the porcelain face of our noble lady. Belgrade—this is also my family, our rose-colored light.

Sanja's had her first child now, a boy named Luka. He's already learned to walk, although none of us from Croatia have seen him in person yet. They bring him to the mirror and teach him his first words—

Say "Luka"
Say "lamp"
Say "table"
Say "ashtray"

He's learning to speak Serbian, surrounded by the relics of our Croatian family history. Before that table witnessed how Luka learned to walk, it belonged to our grandfather's sister. Did she buy it from some estate, some castle? When? After she died, my aunt in Belgrade inherited it. The table rode five hundred kilometers on the back of some truck to get to its new home. A pair of binoculars used to be hidden in its drawers. When I would come to Belgrade, I'd always look for the binoculars in the upper right drawer to find them one more time, but they had been stolen long before the table had even been brought to the city.

Above the table hangs a portrait of my great-grandmother. She's wearing her sleeping cap, already looking quite old. The painting, oil on leather, was done by her son, Jakob Socher, who had studied art in Munich. So many decades have passed, but the portrait has kept her among us. In a certain sense, every trip to Belgrade was also somehow a trip to our Croatian great-grandmother.

Uncle Jakob never finished art school, but became a land surveyor instead. He never even framed the painting and to this day the portrait hangs unframed. An artist who had pledged my aunt to get the picture framed died before he could fulfill his promise.

Next to the portrait is a light brown plate, mounted on the wall, also with some sort of painting on its surface. Time has nibbled away at the image. Every time I visited Belgrade, I would stare at the plate, trying in vain to decipher its message. Was it a monk bringing some piece of news? Or a stranger trying to lead someone astray?

The ashtray looks like a cast-iron grape leaf. Gray, with some sort of dried flower pressed into it. Perhaps an edelweiss. It used to be in the middle of my great-grandfather's small bamboo side table, but somehow I managed to get this latter object for myself. The *Rauchtisch*, as we call it in my family—German for "smoking table." I, as the oldest granddaughter, successfully begged for the table from my grandmother. "Well, if you insist," she said. And I insisted.

Everything that used to be on the table is now in Belgrade. When we meet, the ashtray will sit once more on the *Rauchtisch*. It's been a long time since they've been in the same room.

I was last in Belgrade in September 1991. War already thundered with her full-throated canons. I was coming back from Iran. Flights between Belgrade and Tehran still operated. Between Belgrade and Zagreb, not any more. The two points on that path had become enemies and between them lay a warzone.

My uncle met me at the airport. We drove past a crowd of men waiting for something. I could just make out the head of the line.

"What are they waiting for? Gasoline?"

He paused a while before giving a terse reply.

"No. Those are the volunteers."

My head was still floating among the saffron and turquoise domes of Isfahan. "Volunteers for *what*?" I almost asked, but, quickly, I understood. In those lines stood men going off to fight the war against Croatia. I watched a pair of hands. Their fingers took a cigarette out from its crumpled pack. Fingers that would soon pull a trigger. A helicopter flew overhead. My eyes darted from the men back to my uncle. Looking at him, the war no longer existed.

My uncle wanted to say something, but didn't know how to start.

Two more helicopters were flying above us.

"Those helicopters are taking wounded soldiers from the battlefield." Belgrade's hospitals were full of men maimed by Croatian bullets, fingers, hands. "It's a real bad situation. Yesterday there was some shooting in Varaždin."

Varaždin, my hometown. My parents. My first Esperanto lessons. *Kolombo estas birdo, leono estas besto.* In Varaždin was the second half of those ashtrays and tables that now lived with me in Zagreb.

It was impossible to drive from Belgrade to Croatia. I'd have to get to Hungary, and only from there, circle around back home.

When we got to my uncle's apartment in Belgrade, the television was broadcasting news from his native Gospić in Croatia. The Croats had hung six Serbs, or so TV Beograd told us. From a white bottle, Uncle took out a small round pill. He said nothing.

In my mind I saw that pot of food, half a century earlier, that couldn't be delivered to his imprisoned father. I had no white bottle on hand. My parents were in Varaždin, where yesterday bullets began to fly.

The table was strewn with leftovers, my favorite Serbian delicacies. "I'm leaving my pajamas under the pillow, so I'll have something to wear on my next surprise visit." They appreciated my optimism. None of us cried, not even Luka—he wasn't yet able. Sanja and I took him for a walk by the water. Relaxed, growing in her belly, he was waiting patiently to be born. We looked out over the Sava River, which flows through Zagreb before it reaches Belgrade.

After I left, it wasn't possible to call or send letters directly back to Belgrade. One letter, sent to Croatia through Hungary, came with a photo of Luka, just a few months old. We marveled at his bright, alert eyes, and tried to imagine the face of his father, whom none of the Croatian relatives had ever met.

"Look how much we have to gain when we refuse to hate!" wrote my aunt courageously in one letter.

We told them about the celebrations we had for our grand-mother's ninetieth birthday, listing the guests and detailing the menu. In Belgrade, they knew who sat where in our living room. They could guess from which glasses we drank and picture the garlands that decorated the edges of our special dishes. "And Auntie's cake for dessert!" Sanja saw the turn-of-the-century cake platter before her with its pattern of painted cherries peeking out from under the crumbs of the last piece.

When I left Belgrade, my uncle accompanied me to the bus station and looked at me through the window, sitting and ready to go to the other side, to Croatia. I smiled at him. He did not return my smile, but just looked at me for a long time, saying goodbye with his eyes.

Now, when I hear those declarations that we must throw bombs on Belgrade, I see that look of farewell on my uncle's face. And if bombs do fall on that city, don't think about the porcelain lamp, Sanja. Grab Luka and run to the bomb shelter.

We, here on the other side, are waiting for the message that you are still alive.

**In *Mars, God of Croatia* (1922), Miroslav Krleža wrote
the following on the nature of power:**

The captain never listened to anyone who said that power could be wielded dishonestly, immorally, or stupidly. That it could come in despicable, tyrannical, or barbarous forms. Quite the contrary! To him, power stirs up bright and cheerful feelings like those borne by simple-minded children staring at the naked blade of a sword shining in the sunlight. The child is enamored with the nickel-plated blade and thinks to himself—why not use it to cut and slice while it's still all sharp and silvery? The captain regards his power through these child's eyes and uses his authority with joy and gusto, swinging it around like the child with his naked, sharp blade. When the captain yells "Company right! March!" he has no idea that his shouting is the fulfillment of a scheme hatched in the Middle Ages by some shadowy organization, the same organization that tries to sell its wares from Thessaloniki to Baghdad. Those sorts of conspiracy theories are printed in the opposition newspapers, the kind that no decent person reads. But the captain isn't aware that he is in fact a cog in the black machine, an unthinking, primitive, gigantic machine. Many years of training have dulled his half-intelligent, sluggish mind and ravaged his desolate, uncultivated soul. Those long years of training spring from the captain's mouth with an amplified shriek, spouting programmatic nonsense.

On the use of Catholic symbols on Croatian military uniforms:

Christ does not hang upon the breast of the patriotic soldier like the symbol of an idea. Christ has become a barbarian fetish that soldiers condemned to death pin onto their filthy shirtfronts to protect themselves against the firing squad or the hangman's noose. Even in the Malay Archipelago, men paint themselves blood red and take statues of their gods into the battlefield as protection against impending death. Apart from his oleographed Christ, each soldier tucks a picture of Mary Mother of God of Bistrica inside the rim of his cap, or carries the image of Saint Roch in his pocket. In Croatia, there is more than The One True God. There are many, an endless number of Croatian gods... Practically the entire detachment has been dedicated to innumerable saints, beatified holy men, and guardian angels. And many of those condemned soldiers, who naively went off to rob, burn, slaughter, and murder, will crawl back on their bare knees to the sacrificial altar and lick the church marble, convinced that their necks had been saved, if they returned alive at all, by the luminous blessings of the Almighty. Back at the base, a huge Croatian flag hangs in the window in three rain-soaked colors, with a large head of Christ crudely and frighteningly added in paint. Faded and drenched, Christ's face is distorted into a demonic grin, almost like the melancholy Pantokrator of Byzantine frescoes.

ALARM

Trucks were transporting sand and pouring it out in high mounds on the sidewalk. My neighbors in the apartment building were filling old sacks with it. They placed the sandbags in front of the basement windows to protect them. *To protect them from what?*

"From the debris of the bombing hurtling towards our homes."

The reality of that sentence erased any illusions.

Neighbors, who in more civil times barely said hello to one another, now helpfully passed each other shovels. The sacks were originally destined for something else—their contents should have been sugar. On a few of them you could still make out the English words *SUGAR, Product of Nigeria* or *Product of Yugoslavia.* A few bore Chinese ideograms. The bags leaned on every basement window, covering them up like thick curtains. If a window was relatively high off the ground, the heavy bags were put on top of a table or on a makeshift foundation of bricks. Then the sandbags were piled one atop the other, like heaps of slaughtered pigs. The sidewalks narrowed in the face of these intruders. Several of the sacks tore while being carried over to the windows and from these holes tiny streams of sand cascaded, as if trying to save themselves from the great hourglass of war.

From the radio came the recommendation to clean out our basements. Neighbors got rid of forgotten mattresses and three-legged chairs, unusable cookware and empty bottles. All sorts of junk accumulated on the sidewalk, awaiting garbage collectors. The basement in my building smelled like mold and sadness. Thick cobwebs drooped down from the ceiling. Within the basement, each resident had their own small cellar, usually a place to keep trash. Those who heated their homes in the winter with coal or wood kept their spare supplies down there, along with an anvil-shaped tree stump for chopping logs. The back wall of each of the cells was made of thin wooden slats, already rotten with age, especially where they met the cement floor. There, rats gnawed and forced their way inside.

Before reaching the individual cellars there was a sort of common "antechamber," a low-ceilinged concrete room with a door leading out to the back garden. This antechamber was declared the official bomb shelter for all the residents of the building. A few city bureaucrats came by to ensure that the space conformed to construction regulations. They certified it a useable shelter and affixed the official symbol of refuge—a blue triangle on an orange background—to the outer door.

On the street, everyone would stop at every corner and check quickly for those signs, just in case. *Where's the bomb shelter?* When the sirens sounded everyone would rush inside as fast as possible. We all dreamed of reaching the refuge closest to home, but were often detained for hours in strange and uncomfortable shelters.

Some shelters were in underground stores, cafés, or clubs. We felt that the refuge in our building was sufficiently luxurious—we even had our own bathroom.

I was making a pot of tea on a Sunday afternoon when the sirens howled. I had been out of the country the week before, so while my neighbors were already desensitized, I was overcome with a sudden dread, tying knots in the pit of my stomach.

I grabbed a mug and put it in the bag, which I had prepared as soon as I got back from abroad. To welcome me home, my relatives had called, instructing me to pack a bag and leave it by the door to my apartment. It seemed as though everyone was preparing for a long trip away from the city. Or away from their normal lives. And into the war.

In the bag there was a flashlight, my documents, my wallet, a pair of warm socks, a shawl, a sweater, a box of crackers, a bottle of water, a plastic cup, and a book about Isfahan that I was reading. Folded on top was a woolen blanket, an essential part of life in the basement. I shoved a thermos, full of hot tea, into the bag, which clinked against the small box with family heirlooms I'd hidden.

Was there still time to use the bathroom before going downstairs?

"Quick! Didn't you hear the siren?" My neighbor was already nervously ringing the doorbell.

I had heard it. But I was slow. It was my first time hearing the siren. My hands were shaking. I grabbed the thickest coat from the closet. It won't be so warm sitting for hours in the basement. I put on winter boots. In the doorway I turned and looked back, my heart tearing, at the home I was leaving behind. The apartment was somehow beautiful, as things can be when we say goodbye to them, peaceful and offering the promise of security. This was the place where, in every way, I was most strongly myself. But now it was dangerous. I was being forced to leave.

Will I return? Will I be able to find it again?

Any envy I felt for those in happier parts of the world, who have the right to stay at home, was cut short. My neighbor on the staircase was hyperventilating. She was elderly, released from the hospital just a few months ago, after a stroke.

"Leave your bag. I'll take it. Go. Hurry. Just get downstairs. Please, go!"

Our downstairs neighbors preferred to flee to an actual anti-ballistic blast shelter a few buildings away. We decided to stay in our basement, in that rats' nest, which I would have darted through in better times on the way to the back garden. I couldn't stand its dank and humid air. And now this place was to be our sanctuary.

By the time I got down there, the room was already full. My neighbors knew each other from a distance at best, but we now spoke to each other warmly, full of concern for one another.

"If this goes on any longer, we'll need to bring down some boards and cover up the concrete. The cold is coming in from over there."

"I'll give you my old rugs. You can hang them on the walls."

And so it began. We sat with blankets draped over our laps, sinking into our uncomfortable chairs. These chairs had been thrown down here for a reason after all. It wasn't too long before the bolts in the chair backs felt like they were boring into our spines. I began to make a mental list of all the things

I'd need to bring down from my apartment to make life underground more bearable. If the next bombing didn't raze the building, I could, for example, bring down a few more armchairs. There'd even be space for a full recliner, if we'd have to spend the night. My fur scarf would be good too. A few hours sitting here, I thought, and I'll soon be longing for warmth.

I resisted the urge to walk around the shelter since any movement would mess with the reception of our transistor radio. One of the women from my building had brought it down and was constantly fiddling with it so we could hear the news. The station broadcast music after which it announced that our city's air raid alert was still in effect.

"Those idiots are playing music at a time like this!" she grumbled.

"The idiots are the ones in the airplanes!" her husband corrected. Complaining about the radio program could be interpreted as a critique of the government itself. An announcer interrupted the music to tell us that the alert was now in force for seven other towns near the capital, towns clustered like links in a chain, whose frightened citizens were now abandoning their homes and rushing down into their cellars and basements. In one of these towns, the sirens would sound nineteen times in a single day.

No one wanted to drink my tea. Instead, the neighbors loudly debated what the total number of causalities was for the day, adding up the figures they had heard on the morning news. I kept quiet in the face of their calculations and strained my ears to listen for other sounds. If they kept on at this volume, we'd miss the all-clear siren.

"That's not a good place," my neighbor remarked. "You're sitting too close to the stairs. That's the weakest point. If something happens, you won't be safe."

He was right. I had positioned myself as close as possible to the exit. From there, the strongest memories of life came down to us. Now the street lamps were snuffed out; the city was dead.

But it was still alive under the earth. There it breathed and there it waited.

I don't know exactly how many times the citizens of Zagreb had to retreat into their basements. A few people in nearby buildings put a notch in the wall every time they went down to the shelter. Rumor has it that the number of notches went no higher than fifty. In total, no more than seventy hours of subterranean living. Zagreb was lucky. Aerial bombings had hit the city only three times. Two times they hit the television tower on the mountain next to the city. One time they hit the presidential palace, not far from my home. All the other times we hid, we just sat afraid and listened to the canons firing in the distance. Twenty-five kilometers to the south of the city was the frontline.

An overwhelming desire to return home prevented me from thinking about anything else. The tension broke—it was clear that I would get out of there that day. It seemed that sometimes the airplanes were flying around just sight-seeing. No detonations could be heard.

Another neighbor started talking about the dead rat they found on their first time down in the shelter. I gazed nervously around the room. "Our friend's booming voice must have scared off all the other rats," I said trying to reassure myself. "The dead ones had already been disposed of".

The radio started to play one of those songs designed to whip up our patriotism. It sounded disgustingly primitive, glorifying the "unconquerable Croats" and crudely rhyming "nation" and "foundation".

"It must be something really bad if they're playing *Hrvatine* again," the neighbor observed. He was always paying special attention for the secret messages in the broadcasts.

The clock showed that we had been in the basement for all of seventeen minutes. I took out my book about Isfahan and looked for the section about the city's famed Swinging Minarets, an architectural wonder built on the gravesite of a 14th century mystic. According to legend, when a visitor enters one minaret, he can, through the vibrations of his own body, shake the structure's second minaret as well. After the bombing of Isfahan, the minarets no longer reacted to a visitor's movements. I read those sentences twice, but understood nothing about the mosque and its miraculous towers. A frightened mind, a loud neighbor, a blaring radio, the nation rhymed with foundation—this wasn't exactly the best atmosphere for reading about Iranian architecture.

"What do you think? How will this all end?" the neighbor wanted to hear my opinion.

"I'm no prophet, sir. We'll see."

This neighbor, who lived in a basement room even when the alert wasn't in effect, declared that he would get a gun for himself, no matter how much it cost. He was forced to live in a sunless cellar apartment on account of his many, many financial problems. But he had his priorities. A weapon gave him a much stronger sense of security than his desiccated dwellings could. Before he could present all the details on the going prices for firearms, the all-clear siren sounded. It was the same sound that had cast us down into the basement, but this time it was cause for our collective joy and relief. It seemed as though the end of the war itself had been announced.

Afterwards, we grew accustomed and apathetically accepted it: the first siren, which invites us down to the basement, always announces that the world has come to an end. The next siren, which calls us back from below, announces that it has been saved.

"Are you going to leave your quilts down here? We might have to come right back down"

"Don't draw the devil on the wall! You're inviting bad luck!"

The devil had already been drawn. Mars, the Devil in Croatia.

I carried my blankets and my neighbor's blankets, her bag and my bag, and stumbled in the darkness on the staircase. My flashlight wasn't working. The city was a ghastly black, its lights extinguished after the first sounding of the alarm. I flew upwards, towards the third floor, towards home.

I threw down my neighbor's things at her door, said goodnight, and fumbled trying to get my key into the lock. The door opened. The familiar smell of home engulfed me. Still in the hallway, I stood and felt a simple and pure joy. The pleasure of home, mild and calming.

But happiness is not to be savored. Quick, to the bathroom. During wartime, the bathroom is a holy chamber. A blessed room. To get reacquainted with the scent of one's soap is one of life's greatest delights. To see how water flows from the faucet! To see that little yellow flame burn under the hot water heater!

My books and my paintings silently awaited my return. We greeted each other with quiet enthusiasm, as after a long absence.

I craved soup. Soup with a hearty broth, thick with vegetables. I took out a pot from the cabinet. It clattered and banged as I took it off the shelf, but the noise couldn't disguise the greater clamor—the siren rang out again.

Quick. Now. Go. Shut off the gas. Check the water. Put on the boots. Button the jacket.

My neighbor's voice was already echoing angrily.

"Where are you? Don't you hear the siren?!"

I was grateful for this short pause that brought me home again and taught me a lesson about happiness.

Around midnight, when the siren once again announced a halt to the danger, my key, completely independent and of its own free will, unlocked the door to my apartment in total darkness.

Exhausted, I threw myself fully clothed onto the bed. My pillow felt dishonestly soft as my boots stood at attention at the edge of the bed, ready to take my feet and flee into the night.

RENÉ FROM VUKOVAR

"Is this the Esperanto Center?"

"Yes. Please come in."

"Can I speak with you? I'm René's aunt. René, from Vukovar. You know that René's disappeared. We've been looking for him, trying to find him any way we can—the Red Cross, Amnesty International, the Croatian Army Commission on Disappeared Persons. There's no sign of him."

The words cascaded from the woman's mouth. She still remembered how to speak Esperanto. She wasn't thinking of the famed role that the Universal Esperanto Association played during the First World War. She was reacting instinctively. Esperanto is international. It must be able to do more than these rigid institutions.

René from Vukovar. Vukovar—the new symbol of our destruction. The war's most suffering victim for whom Yugoslavia ended its seventy-three year existence. The easternmost city in Croatia, on the Danube, decimated by grenades during weeklong battles. Vukovar's bombed-out hospital was the site of the city's last pulse of life. For weeks, neither medicine nor food could reach the city. Its wounded and its children, its pregnant women and its elderly—despite the efforts of international organizations, none of them could be evacuated. The roads into Vukovar had been turned into minefields, impossible to approach.

In these cruel battles, international norms of conduct are no longer observed. This is a war where the flag of the Red Cross is shot like a bullseye. Those shots are fired from the guns of the Yugoslav Army and Serb extremists, those who are convinced that only guns can prevent the democratic dissolution of Yugoslavia, or can stop Croatia, once an integral part of that country, from becoming an independent state. The will of the voters isn't important. Let the guns decide.

For days on end, those of us who lived in more peaceful regions listened to the news of Vukovar's suffering. The siege. The massacre of people defending the city. The destruction of its most important buildings. A shortage of blood plasma in the hospital. A shortage of— Day after day, each broadcast more terrible than the last. If we in Zagreb heard the air raid sirens only twice in one day or spent only a few days in our basements, we were ashamed to leave our shelters knowing that the people of Vukovar wouldn't be able to leave their cellars for weeks. To go draw water from the well meant death. To go bury your bullet-ridden neighbor in the closest garden similarly meant to lie yourself down dead next to him.

The half-destroyed hospital was set up as a refuge for survivors who had lost their homes. How could one live in those ruined buildings? Under the earth, in their cellars and basements, in underground shelters, the inhabitants struggled to survive. One story more horrific than the next. You couldn't spread butter on your toast in the morning without your conscience gnawing: how can you do this in Zagreb when people were starving in Vukovar?

Before the war began in 1991, Vukovar was a small city in eastern Croatia with no more than forty thousand inhabitants and a port on the Danube. The small river Vuka, itself a tributary of the Danube, gave the city its name. The city is located near Fruška Gora, a mountain home to many varieties of wine. More than once have I toasted to life over its famed wines. And during those toasts it never mattered to anyone whether it was Serbian or Croatian wine we were drinking.

Now it seems like the whole planet has been divided into Serbs and Croats—hatred has risen like a flood and no one has bothered to build a dam. They, the others, are to blame. They, the others, are the destroyers. Each side accuses the other. Watered with memories of old grudges, new hatreds have sprouted all around.

Under socialism, such hatred was forbidden in Yugoslavia. The peoples of the country coexisted peacefully, or so everyone was taught. The official motto "fraternity and unity" was, by force of law, on everyone's lips. More than one person was sent to prison for expressing too strong an admiration for his own nation or for too strongly cursing against another.

When the regime changed, slander against other groups became the rule. Newly founded political parties hungrily accumulated arguments to explain why and just how badly the other nations had exploited their people. The pot began to boil. The pressure cooker exploded.

After the fall of communism, the Croats rediscovered their Croatianness with great joy. And they remembered all the painful times they had not been allowed to live fully as ethnic Croats. Once they discovered the roots of this mistreatment, they made sure the story was spread as far and wide as possible. It was the fault of the previous regime, so the story went, who had given out privileges only to the few and persecuted all the others. "Serbs enjoyed exclusive rights. Croats were oppressed" the Croats declared. "The only privileged ones were the Croats themselves" argued the Serbs. All who dared mention that life wasn't all bad under the old regime were glared at with a specific sort of look: "There goes an enemy of the people!" More considerate folk thought these supposed enemies were simply near-sighted, unable to acknowledge the crimes of the past. The spark of dispute was ready to ignite. Fights began between family members, spouses, friends. Tolerance fled elsewhere, somewhere where people knew how to make space for it.

Vukovar is the easternmost city in Croatia, located in the region of Slavonia. On the other side of the Danube, Serbia begins. When the war began in 1991, the city of Vukovar suddenly became a point of grave strategic importance. It's a small place, made famous on account of a clay dove. An ancient ritual artifact, the renowned dove is a work of art dating back from sometime between the Neolithic Era and the Bronze Age, discovered in 1938 at the Vučedol archaeological site near Vukovar. Consisting of painstakingly glued-together small pieces, it can now be seen in the Archaeological Museum in Zagreb. When the war broke out, the museums put all of their greatest treasures in basement shelters. The Vučedol Dove probably lies carefully packed away in some box. She spends the war better protected than the citizens of Vukovar itself: already shattered long ago, nothing will happen to her in the present conflict.

It is truly a breathtaking archaeological treasure. I've marveled many times at the oblique, angular carvings on the dove's earthen neck and breast. The dove is a symbol of peace. Vukovar is a symbol of conflict. Heavy winged, the dove has fled through the smoke of the smoldering city of Vukovar. A bird of peace thousands of years old, shot down. At the time when it seems that the bloody twentieth century is finally giving way to the twenty-first, the Balkan passion for primitive weaponry has been reawakened.

Vukovar also has its paragraph in the history of Esperanto in Yugoslavia. In 1922, the city hosted the Second Congress of the Socialist Labor Party, where a special resolution on Esperanto was adopted. The resolution was presented to the Congress by a university professor, Dr. Radomir Andonivič, in the name of the Communist Esperanto Club of Belgrade. According to the resolution, "the Congress will consider all Communist Esperanto groups on the territory of Yugoslavia as affiliates of the Party". As a result of this successful agitation, the Congress proposed that all Party branches and syndicates morally support local Esperanto groups and help them organize activities, events, presentations, and courses on and about Esperanto among the proletariat. Along the same lines, the Congress in Vukovar also recommended that all Party and syndicate newspapers give Esperantists space in their pages.

I have never been to Vukovar.

Several months before the war began, René wrote to our Esperanto Center in Zagreb to ask if someone might be able to come and give a presentation about the language sometime after "the situation" quieted down. Back then we used the word "situation" to describe the constant state of chaos that swirled around us. The situation back then was typified by a few bombings here and there on the railroad tracks that ran from Belgrade to Zagreb and Zagreb to Belgrade. It had suddenly become dangerous to travel on several railway lines. We would wait for the situation to calm down.

Soon it was impossible to travel by train in any direction. The situation sharpened.

We listened to the news, our stomachs turning to stone. The "situation" had decided to cast us out from our former, fleeting lives. Cruelty moved into our thoughts and invaded our senses.

Lucky were those who didn't have a television. My eyes held onto the memory of more serene times longer than others—I didn't spend my nights watching atrocities on the screen. I only heard about them on the radio. The ears are more superficial than the eyes. In the morning, I could not yet tell whether what I heard had really been the truth or just some horrible nightmare.

"I'll go to Vukovar as soon as it's possible. In the autumn." I said that summer, René's invitation in my hand.

I never made that visit to Vukovar. The autumn never came to Vukovar either. A deadly summertime frost had already ravaged the city.

"When did he disappear?"

"November 17th, 1991. They entered the city and…"

Who entered the city? This was not a question one really needed to raise. We heard about the horrors in Vukovar every day. "Vukovar" was the word with which the morning news began. "They" were the Serb extremists, the White Eagles, the followers of Šešelj or Arkan or whatever they called those monsters who thought that military campaigns could solve everything.

The Serbs nursed an image of their history deeply immersed in myth. They had convinced themselves of the idea that anywhere in Yugoslavia where Serbs lived was in fact Serbia itself. As it was in Vukovar, so it was later in parts of Bosnia. These places were targeted in Serbian campaigns that sought to defend the local "endangered" Serbs. From Belgrade's perspective, it was necessary to liberate the "transplanted Serbs," that is, the Serbs who lived in republics other than Serbia. And this is how the catastrophe at Vukovar came to pass: to liberate a city meant to destroy it.

Vukovar has been liberated! announced the newspapers in Belgrade.

Vukovar has fallen! cried the Croatian newscasters.

Fallen into enemy hands. Liberated by the heroes. Two expressions for the destruction of Vukovar.

What did it mean to liberate a city if it no longer existed?

Could Esperanto help find René? I'd not yet given up hope. I liked to believe that Esperanto could.

I messaged the headquarters of the Universal Esperanto Association in Rotterdam.

Rotterdam responded kindly and promptly that the relatives of the missing person, rather than his fellow Esperantists, needed to fill out a questionnaire with all its attendant details in order to submit a formal request to search for the missing person. *What is the Last Known Address of the Missing Person(s)?* read one question. *Božidara Adžije 36* I wrote sadly, trying to imagine a building with the roof still intact and glass still in the windowpanes. *What is the Last Known Telephone Number of the Missing Person(s)?* Such precise European bureaucracy! Try and call that number and find out what's happening! Is it not grotesque to ask for these phone numbers? These people are coming from bombed-out cities where even the postal service stopped functioning months ago.

I remember my last visit to René. He'd already married Nevena. They'd just moved to Zadar, her native city. Both of them had trained as dentists and moved into her grandmother's house while looking for work. Positions were few. René cooked, she complained. The third bottle of oregano this week for his delicacies! He could not get in the habit of measuring out his ingredients from the spice bottles in the cabinet. Grandma's doilies hung over every surface.

I had met them at an Esperanto club meeting in Zagreb when we were all still students. They were quite affectionate with one another.

"*Too* affectionate. This won't end well."

In Zadar, their wedding photo hung by the mirror. How young they looked! She on his shoulder. He, a gentleman in a white suit and white gloves.

I held the photo in my hand. I liked the image very much.

"We're already beating each other up," René commented on his first year of marriage. There was still love hidden in his eyes as he turned to her. "Our guest thinks that I'm speaking meta-phorically."

The whole time I was in their home, a welcome poster hung on the wall in my honor.

She had a certain grace. Their life was still good-hearted, the darkness yet unseen. On holidays, he still took the tie from his wedding suit out of the closet.

They showed me their wedding gifts. One was a porcelain replica of the Vučedol Dove. It had broken in transit from his city to hers. "Now it looks more like the real thing," quipped René. Their reglued dove did indeed bear a stronger than usual resemblance to its Neolithic counterpart.

I found out about their divorce only afterwards. He found work in Žegar, a small village where "God says goodnight," in the vicinity of Zadar. Not far from the village was the Krupa Monastery, an Orthodox church and an outstanding example of Serbian art in the region. The locals took to René quickly. Nowadays it's necessary to say that he was beloved by both the Serbs and the Croats of the region. René—who had grown up in a Croat Catholic family—was often invited to have din-ner with the Serbian Orthodox Bishop. He started collecting regional idioms and even began to write in the local dialect. He sent a long letter to us in Zagreb filled with vulgar, yet witty and nuanced village expressions. He told how he had the best dentist's office in the region, seeing as how he knew all the lat-est techniques and had mastered all the latest instruments. I didn't save the letter. I had no idea it would be his last.

From Žegar, René moved back to Vukovar. He found a po-sition in the dental practice at the rubber factory in the nearby town of Borovo. His brother, four years his elder, worked along -side him.

By the middle of September 1991, it was no longer advisable to drive from Vukovar to Borovo—to leave the house meant to be in the line of fire and to put one's life in constant danger.

The home in which René lived with his brother, Robert, and their mother was a family-owned property left to them by his grandfather Jan, an ethnic Czech who sold agricultural machinery. The machines sold well in the agrarian region of Slavonia, and in the city center their family home grew with their prosperity. It looked a bit like a castle. Their wealthy grandfather decorated it with carefully selected oaken furniture.

In September 1991, grenades shattered every window in the house and damaged the roof. During a half-hour lull in the shooting the brothers climbed up to the roof and tried to protect their home with plaster. Then the rains came, dense and cold. The cellar was, fortunately, strong and secure.

One day an oak desk suddenly took flight and slammed through the bathroom wall. No one was injured. Everyone had been in the cellar when the house was hit.

For decades, their grandfather's grape vines had crawled up the bars of the iron gate that surrounded the courtyard. A grenade ripped the bars out from the cement and flung them onto a neighbor's lawn.

It was the middle of September when René's aunt last spoke with him. For hours, she dialed all the numbers she knew in Vukovar trying to reach her relatives in the besieged city. The overloaded phone lines prohibited family members, longing for contact, to get in touch with their relatives. Levelled by bombs, the post offices no longer functioned.

All of a sudden, she succeeded. She could hear clearly how the telephone echoed in Grandpa Jan's great house. No response. Lost in thought, she let the phone ring. Unexpectedly, René picked up. He grumbled, complaining against those who would wake up their sleeping relatives during one of their brief nighttime breaks from the shooting. His typical wit and spirit, renowned within the family and outside it, was beginning to wither. In his voice, one could hear the pain—there was no exit from this situation. He felt isolated in the isolated city of Vukovar.

This was how René's aunt interpreted the conversation in retrospect, after she had understood that this was the last time she would get to speak with her nephew.

Later it was no longer possible to call Vukovar.

It had seemed then that Vukovar was the Croatian Hiroshima. But after the fall of the city, it seemed like so much of the country had become Vukovar.

We heard about René's last day from his brother Robert.

The 17th of November was the high point of the Vukovar tragedy. A round of bullets followed by several knocks on the door. The dog jumped. Robert opened the door.

One of the gunmen had deep lines on his face. He wore a uniform. A beard. A red star on his cap. A white ribbon on his shoulder, the symbol of the White Eagles. Two grenades hung from his belt. And a knife. He held his rifle in his hands.

"How many people are here?"

"Three" said Robert soberly.

The language wasn't foreign. Besides a few variations, it was the same. This was a war in which the aggressor and the victim could understand each other very well. No interpreter necessary.

"You have three minutes to vacate this building"

The family wasn't ready to leave. No one had believed that the worst would happen. And yet it had.

The brothers had prepared their dental diplomas earlier. They didn't need to look for them. This was something they had needed to have with them even in basement.

René handed his mother her shoes. In the excitement, he took the wrong ones, her Dutch-made slippers that she wore around the house. She instinctively refused the slippers and put on her boots. A stroke of luck.

Outside, on the other side of the glassless windows, it was November.

Their mother quickly grabbed the family's box of gold and jewelry, but her hand went straight from the box to thinking about food. She managed to shove a pair of long sausages into her bag. Later she realized that in her haste she took the wrong box, taking instead the one next to the valuables, the box filled with beads. The gold stayed at home, along with the house's greatest work of art—Grandpa Jan's marvelous old style fireplaces. As she came to the front steps, she realized that she'd forgotten her eyeglasses.

"My glasses" she said to the uniform, wanting to go back inside.

"Your glasses or your life. Take your pick. Clear enough for you?"

She didn't go back.

She wasn't allowed to turn around. That might aggravate him. She sped up.

Coming towards them was a woman from the neighboring street. She had had more than three minutes to pack. Loaded with multiple bags, she stumbled. René's mother ran ahead to help the fallen woman.

"Where do you think you're going?" growled the uniform.

"Don't, Mama, he'll shoot! Don't go!" That was René's voice.

The civilians were gathered together and brought en masse to the Velepromet storage facility.

"Are there Serbs here?"

This was the first way the group was divided. Take the Serbs out from the rest.

Silence.

"Are there any Serbs here?"

Two women announced themselves and were taken away. The non-Serbs remained.

The second way the group was divided was according to sex. Family members were separated. The men who had been led away turned over wine crates in the warehouses and sat down. It was clear that they would be waiting a long time. One day, maybe two. Without food, without water.

The boxes on which the men sat were made for wine bottles, for those famous wines with a picture of the clay dove on the label.

From time to time someone would enter the dark warehouse and abruptly shine a flashlight on the prisoners' faces. Fear. Eyes squinting, blinded by the light.

Repeatedly, they called the prisoners in one by one for questioning. Would the prisoners ever come back?

What time was it when the man called René's name? He was called as one of three, rather than alone. With him were two officials from the wine industry, the director of distribution and the city vinologist. René put on his glasses and was taken to the door. Eyelids heavy, Robert caught a glimpse of his brother in his peripheral vision. At the door, a ray of light shined from the outside. A scream. Robert recognized René's voice. There was no doubt. René had cried out. A howl. The last sound his brother would make that would ever reach his ears.

Shots were heard immediately after the scream.

None of the three came back to the warehouse.

That night the brothers' friend in the warehouse tried to slit his wrists with a crooked piece of sheet metal. He was stopped. Some hours later, his name was called. He never returned.

On the third day, Robert was taken to the barracks outside Vukovar. There, for the first time, water and bread were distributed. A box of sardines. A slice of bread. Their last meal had been eaten at home three days before. Breakfast.

The International Red Cross acted as an intermediary between Zagreb and Vukovar. Relatives in Zagreb waited for the buses to arrive with people from Vukovar. Many came back as a result of population exchanges—so many Croats for so many Serbs.

René's aunt stood at attention waiting for each bus. A quick glance at each of the crumpled faces. No one familiar. Day after day, a new bus filled with survivors. A hopeful insomnia—maybe in tomorrow's transport…

"Your nephew is alive. He bandaged my wounds in the camp," reported one man from Vukovar.

The comfort of those words warmed her waiting.

How many buses did she wait for? She held photos of her three missing relatives—René, Robert, and their mother—at the ready in her handbag. "Have you seen them?" The question repeated itself endlessly.

Her sister, the boys' mother, turned up on November 22nd dressed in the jumpsuit she had been wearing the day the White Eagle knocked on her door. René's aunt had left her house that morning later than usual and drove to the hotel where the bus would bring the survivors from Vukovar. It was freezing outside and her car hadn't wanted to start. René's mother, coatless, stepped off the bus and met her sister's gaze. They looked at each other through tears. Only afterwards, at home, surrounded by familiar objects, could the mother begin to talk. It would take her hours to explain what they had been through.

The hopeful waiting continued. Eighteen days later, from a bus filled with people brought in exchange for Serbs, Robert emerged. René's scream was still visible on his face. The aunt thawed out his frozen spirit with the warmth of family.

They waited for every subsequent bus of refugees from Vukovar. René wasn't in any of them. Neither was his name on any list of dead, wounded, or imprisoned.

No one has ever found René.

Many returnees planted seeds of hope: someone saw him in the camp in Stajićevo, others in Niš, three people saw him in Banjica. A few claimed that they heard his "yes" during a roll call.

The women prayed.

God, thank you for saving one boy. Bring back the other one from wherever he is.

He disappeared in November 1991.

In February we celebrated his birthday without any hint of him.

Summer gallops closer.

At night, an uncertain idea awakens us.

Scream.

Hope.

RECRUITMENT

Today my brother was called up to the front.

I shoved my hand in the mailbox and took a look at its contents. A very meager harvest today—only newsletters. From France came *Franca Esperantisto* whose front page invited the reader to come plant trees together. On another bulletin there was a stamp bearing the image of the Olympic flame. The lead article was a report on an amusing cabaret that had delighted its audience. In the accompanying photograph, the ladies wore long skirts while knights sported melon-shaped hats.

I belong to those who believe that we are waiting our entire lives for the letter that will change everything. As the writer Milovan Danojlić once put it, "Whenever I see the postman coming down the street, I put all my hope in him. Maybe today he's bringing the great news at long last! Ever since I first became aware of myself, I have been waiting for some sort of redemptive piece of news. The message that will change everything and that will set my life on a new course." I dug my hand into the mailbox one more time to be sure that nothing else was there.

At the back of the mailbox I found a card on which was written: *ORDER TO REPORT FOR MILITARY SERVICE.* It was hard not to just stare at it dumbly. Here it was, the day when everything changes. I had asked for a change, had I not?

The army wanted my brother to report the next day at nine o'clock. The draft card covered up the ladies with their long skirts at the evening cabaret. France cabarets its nights away. I was born here, where a different program is in store. A mix of fear and bitterness suddenly overwhelmed me and wouldn't let me climb the stairs. It was as though I had to carry the whole cast of the cabaret up with me to the third floor. My fingers began to swell, my arms trembled.

My brother and I share an address from the time we used to live together. After he moved in with his girlfriend, he didn't bother to update his address with the ministry of defense. And that's how the war came to my doorstep.

I imagined him at home, newspaper in hand. When I call, he'll reach for the receiver, and never again be able to pick up the thread of the article he's reading. I decided to give him one more hour of peace. I washed my hands for a long time, scrubbing my fingers cleaner than usual. Those fingers that had held the draft papers. The text was the same when I read it again for the tenth time. My brother was expected tomorrow morning at nine o'clock in accordance with his military obligations.

I decided to delay informing him. Let him enjoy life for another ten minutes. I'll call him in another hour.

Should I run away? Where to? To the nightly cabaret? I belong to those who believe that it is not possible to run away from one's problems.

I'd already lost him once before. One day when he was four years old, he disappeared from the house. That afternoon we couldn't find him anywhere. I walked around and around the house calling his name. His ball lay in the yard, but he was nowhere. I wandered the streets, searched every playground, questioned every child. He'd been seen before lunch, but not after that. Nowhere. When my father came back home from work I had to tell him that my little brother had vanished. *But how could he just vanish?* We went looking together, calling out loudly and hopelessly, visiting every store in the neighborhood. He was nowhere to be found. Father grew very angry. I saw my brother's tiny shoes in the hallway and my heart shuddered. Between bouts of anger and anguish, I was suffocated by emotion.

My father discovered him later that evening. He was in the basement along with another small friend of his. They had decided to paint the windows in the basement and hadn't wanted to answer us when we called for him. My brother could tell that coloring in the windows was probably something he wasn't allowed to do. He managed to open the paint buckets, found a brush, and clambered on top of a chair to reach the windows. His friend needed a paintbrush too, so they took a bundle of dry twigs and stuck them onto the end of a pole. Their tools didn't necessarily paint the straightest of lines, but the laws of geometry didn't hold them back.

He stood there, his striped sweater stained in unwashable green paint, and waited for my father's tempest of outrage to subside. His friend ran home, palms painted green, while my brother's chin sank down to his slippers in shame.

No one ever finished painting those windows.

I was so happy that he was back, at home and in the kitchen, but I also felt that I was supposed to get mad at him, at least a little bit. In the family rulebook, it was a great sin not to respond when called for.

"How could you scare us like that?"

He lifted his eyes, his feelings hurt, and refused to answer.

A sad smile spread across my face recalling that incident with my baby brother.

Tomorrow at nine o'clock he will be given a rifle.

Hardly ten minutes had passed. It was silly of me not to have told him immediately. He should make what he wants out of his last free night. I'll go call him now!

I felt faint. I had to drink some water first. How to start so as not to frighten him? So many of his peers have already left for the front. Some enthusiastically. Some out of a sense of duty. The number of casualties meanwhile continues to climb. But there's talk now about the end of hostilities and the soldiers' return. Are new soldiers drafted simply to take the place of their more tired brothers-in-arms? My feet sank into the floorboards just thinking about wearing heavy soldier's boots. Cautiously I wriggled my toes to prove to myself that I didn't have those bulky things on my feet.

My cousin is probably fighting on the other side of the front-line. This isn't just conjecture—why shouldn't he be there? This is after all a civil war and my cousin has lived in our former capital—now the enemy's chief city—since the age of six. My cousin could have been called up with a similar piece of paper written in a similar language, given a uniform and a rifle at nine o'clock some morning, and shown the truck that would take him westward toward some river at the border.

My brother and my cousin haven't seen each for several years. One winter at our grandparents' house they ran one after the other around the table trying to catch each other with home-made lassoes. Grandfather had laid down on the couch for a nap. Suddenly one of the boys ran by and banged him right in the middle of the forehead. Grandfather shot up in surprise and the boys ran off, stifling their laughter. It was up to Grand-mother to discipline the troublemakers.

Will this battle between cousins begin again? Is it not possible to find a more pleasant way to celebrate their reunion?

The last we heard my cousin went into hiding. He won't be found. Others will shoot instead. Not much consolation can be found in that.

Maybe I should listen to the news first? I thought. Maybe some-thing serious has happened and I don't know about it yet.

No, I won't hear the life-changing piece of news on the radio. That piece of news is already here.

I dialed his number. His girlfriend picked up. I told her that I had some bad news. She didn't understand. She didn't want to understand. I had to repeat the horrible information twice. My brother had just stepped out to get a fresh loaf of bread from the store.

In the meantime, I had to try and work as though nothing was going on. On my desk, a book of Korean folktales lay open to the story of Kyonu and Jingnyo. The two lovers were separated, a punishment for disobeying the orders of the Sky King. With the help of the magpies the lovers reunite one day a year, every year. A galaxy of stars, great and deep, divided the lovers.

Where were the magpies now?

Perhaps this translation was not the best choice for tonight's reading.

My brother had visited me just yesterday. It was my birthday. I had wanted to forget about it. During a war, you age several years every month. But he hadn't forgotten. He stood at the door holding an enormous package. *What's in that box?* We opened it together. I didn't quite understand what it was. My brother had a taste for magic tricks. So here was a ladder, but not just any ordinary ladder. When you twisted one of its rungs, it turned into an ironing board.

I had been bothering my brother for two years to put up a light in the basement. For the time being, he hung an extension cord through the window and, if necessary, one could… But, hell, there was a war on—wouldn't it be safer to bring the cable around through the front of the building? He burst out laughing. Indeed, it would be safer if, during a war, there weren't any loose cables about. Then I laughed too. There was so much danger everywhere, and I was worrying about an extension cord. At the beginning of the war, I had called my brother and asked what we were supposed to do with the windows when the air raid siren sounded. I had been out of the country when they explained on TV what to do in case something happened.

"Should I leave the windows open all the way?"

"You can leave them like that. Yes, that's the recommendation." What will we do in the winter, I thought, but then quickly consoled myself with the fact that winter was still far off.

"And the curtains?"

"Don't worry about the curtains. Leave them as you found them and get down to the basement."

I found comfort in his composure. Yesterday he finally fixed that basement light. The cord no longer hung about. A simple *click* and the whole basement was illuminated.

Now I have a light. But what about my brother?

The price for yesterday's repairs was too high.

If I had been just a little less insistent…

What did the fortuneteller do in that Korean tale?

My brother called back. He was back from the store, the loaf of bread still under his arm. He put it down and listened to what I had to tell him.

He asked me to bring the draft card to his office the next day at eight o'clock. I read it to him again. I could picture just how the slanted wrinkles on his brow deepened while he listened.

We'll say goodbye tomorrow at eight o'clock in his office. What is one supposed to say at a sendoff like that?

They say that the first night is the hardest.

I sat back down at my desk and stared at the photograph from the cabaret. One of the knights was bringing his hand up to the side of his half-melon helmet, saluting the viewer.

Who could I turn to at such a terrible time? My address book was overflowing with friends, but I would have to struggle through this night alone.

As I turned out the light, I could hear how the clock hungrily gnawed away at the seconds, one by one.

In 1915, two years before his death, L.L. Zamenhof, the creator of Esperanto, published the following essay excerpted here:

After the War: An Appeal to the Diplomats

A terrible war has now involved almost all of Europe. When an end comes to this mutual mass butchery, which has so disgraced the entire civilized world, the diplomats will assemble and endeavor to reorder relations among the world's peoples. It is to you, to those future overseers of the new world order, to whom I now turn.

When you will come together after the most all-consuming war that history has ever known, you will have before you an extraordinarily great and important task. It will depend upon you whether the world will have an enduring peace that will last a long time, perhaps forever, or whether we will have a temporary silence, soon to be once more interrupted by explosions of interethnic strife or even new wars...

Will you begin to simply redraw and patch up the map of Europe? Will you simply decide that Territory A must be ceded to Nation X and that Territory B must belong to Nation Y? True, such work must be done, but it is the most insignificant portion of your labors. Take care that the redrawing of borders does not become the essence of your undertaking for then your work will have been entirely without value, and the immense bloody sacrifices that the human race has offered will have all been in vain.

However much you desire to satisfy the peoples of the world, however much you endeavor to establish fairness between the various races, you will achieve nothing by redrawing the map, for every apparent act of justice towards one people will, at the same time, be an injustice for another. The current era is not like ancient times: every piece of land worth fighting over has been worked over and soaked with the blood not of one people, but of many; and if you decide that this-or-that territory must belong to this-or-that people, you are not only not being just, but you will also sow in that piece of land the seeds of a future conflict.

The only truly just decision that you can make is thus: to loudly proclaim—as an official, firmly mutually agreed upon and fully guaranteed resolution by all the realms of Europe—the fundamentally natural, but unfortunately until now unobserved principle: that every nation equally belongs, morally and materially, to all of its sons.

It would be much better if, instead of having countries and kingdoms of different sizes, we would have a somehow proportionally and geographically arranged "United States of Europe". But if it is now still too early to discuss this idea, we must at minimum, through the official and mutually agreed upon adoption of this aforementioned principle, do away with that great evil, that eternal font of constant bloodshed, that equates the identity of a state with that of a single ethnic grouping.

When the above principle shall be officially fixed by guaranteed accord of all the nations of Europe, then the chief cause of our wars, of our constant mutual mistrust, and of our endless armament, will disappear because then no one will ever again be able to utter the words "the fatherland is in danger". It is indeed well known that the words "the fatherland is in danger" do not actually signify that someone wants to tear off a piece of our homeland and throw it into the sea, or that someone seeks to rob its inhabitants of their possessions. More commonly these words simply mean that "a threat has arisen in this piece of land, where until now my people have been the masters and other groups only more or less tolerated, that perhaps tomorrow another people will rule and my group will be only a tolerated presence."

I know quite well that enmity between nations will not suddenly vanish within the span of a single day, whatever the arrangement the diplomats might fashion. Yet for this to begin to happen among private persons, in their speech, their schools, and their daily habits, and so on, we are waiting only for you, the diplomats, to give us the opportunity. Mutual hatred between humanity's various peoples is not something natural, just as it is not natural for families from one and the same ethnic group to hate one another. With the exception of our easily remedied inability to understand and know one another, hatred has a single cause— the existence of peoples who dominate and peoples who are dominated, by the blind egoism, arrogance, and mendacity of the former and the natural resistance of the latter. It is easy to make brothers of free and equal men, but it is not possible to make brothers among men when one regards himself as the rightful master over others.

Sinjoroj diplomatoj! After this horrific war of extermination, which has brought the human race down lower than the most savage of beasts, Europe looks to you for peace. It looks not for some short-lived truce, but a consistent peace as is only worthy of our civilized race. But remember, remember, remember, that the only means to achieve this peace is to dispose, once and for all, of the chief cause of all wars—that barbaric remnant of the most ancient times before civilization: the rule of one people over others.

AN ORDINARY DAY

Sparrows were chirping outside my window, talking amongst themselves in a pear tree. What a privilege it was to be woken up by the singing of birds instead of a siren.

In the mailbox, a letter was waiting for me from the gas company letting me know that the cost of gas would soon be rising to 584 times its current price. Not four times, but fivehundredandeightyfour times the current price.

My first stop of the day was the bank, where I had to wait in a long and growing line. The teller wasn't able to give me the amount I requested.

"Only half of that is available," he said.

I stood there dumbfounded. "But I have the full amount in my account!" I protested.

"I am only able to give you half of that sum, Ma'am," the teller said mechanically.

Behind me, the next customer was getting angry.

"But don't you know that we're at war!"

Being at war was like being in a swamp. Or in prison. Or in quicksand. Or in a tomb.

"Give me as much as you can, I'm begging you," I said, finally giving up.

Where did I get the idea that the money in my account was actually mine? No one owns anything anymore. We are at war.

I got to the office late. As I walked in, a young solider stood by the door, unbuttoning the jacket of his uniform. Two similarly uniformed men the same age were standing next to him, whispering to each other in English.

The soldier turned to me, speaking a stilted Esperanto. "Can you help with a delicate matter? Very delicate." He didn't know where to start. "Esperanto might be able to help. I took a few lessons in a beginners' course last year, but never finished because we had to flee. Now I need to get in touch with someone in France."

"What's the matter?"

"I'm coming from the southern front. My friend was killed there. A French citizen. We've come to the capital to bury him. But there's a problem. The Frenchman. We don't know who he is. He was in the French Foreign Legion before he came to us, and used a pseudonym when he joined our ranks. We called him Pierre. But now he's dead and we need to bury him far from home, in what was for him a foreign country. We were good friends and we feel terrible that his family doesn't know that he was killed. But we can't find them. He left his family behind years ago."

"You should get in touch with the embassy. They'll be able to help."

"Right. We did that already, but the officials at the embassy are working very slowly. They won't find the family until later and we have to bury him the day after tomorrow."

"We won't be able to do anything here before then either. What do you know about him? Give me the details."

"His date of birth was…" The soldier knew only the most basic information about his friend, but he knew it by heart.

The two English-speaking soldiers stood in the corner, waiting to see if Esperanto could work more quickly than the world of government officials and bureaucrats.

The telephone rang and interrupted our conversation. It was my lunch hour by the time I was able to get to the *Jarlibro*, an international directory of Esperantists, and locate the right city in France. They were probably sipping wine and eating expensive cheeses, discussing the percentage of fat in each variety.

"We're in need of an unusual bit of assistance. An unidentified French citizen was killed in battle here. We have only scant details about who he was."

"This is a matter for the French Embassy in your country."

"Yes, we know, we've informed the embassy. But the men with whom he served don't want to bury him in a foreign country if it'll be possible to send his remains home. He must be buried the day after tomorrow. The body is under refrigeration until then. If we might be able to find and alert his family, then this soldier won't have to be buried in foreign soil, at least not without letting his relatives know first. Eventually, if it could…"

I kept to the facts, bare and without embellishment. To call overseas was an unimaginable luxury. Whenever someone called from abroad and spoke slowly, I could see the money flying away, one bill after another. How much food could have been bought for the refugees with the money being flushed down the telephone line? Phone calls in a country at war are short and spare. Subject, predicate, object. If it's possible, then do it. If it's not, forget I asked.

My friendly French interlocutor was shocked by my crude and direct manner. In front of him was a piece of fine Brie, 35% fat. And these barbarians were talking about such dreadful things!

"It's incredibly expensive for us to call long distance. If you find something out, let us know. If not, we will bury him here. Thank you and goodbye."

This was ultimately our war. In some sense it felt indecent to bother the outside world and ask that they get involved.

I turned back to the soldiers. "We've done all we can." The young soldier took his jacket and his two compatriots and left. They'll come back tomorrow. If there's no news, they'll go ahead and bury their friend in the military cemetery. The corpse had the right to a space in the morgue until the day after tomorrow. Couldn't they pay for a few more days? Or would that be against regulations? I knew nothing about the politics of storing the dead.

I tried to forget about the morgue and its dead Frenchman. I opened the mail. Some money fell out of the first envelope.

...And please accept this in place of her membership dues for this year. She has died. The funeral was on May 6th. None of us could be there because the war has made it impossible to travel. She had asked that I buy her some books from your libroservo, *but I couldn't make it because of the bombings and because the post office is no longer working in her region...*

She was writing about Iris, a young Bosnian girl. For Iris, who had a heart condition since she was a child, her aunt in

Zagreb was an endless source of Esperanto books and news. The weak-hearted girl had so wanted a 10,000-word Esperanto dictionary, but how could she find such a book in a mining town like Kakanj? So she wrote to her aunt in Zagreb. Her aunt, proud and excited for her niece, took down the order and went searching for the city's Esperanto Center.

"Hello! Do you sell any 10,000-word dictionaries?"

"Yes, those too."

Iris wasn't allowed to travel without someone accompanying her, but she loved to travel nevertheless. Her parents didn't let her go more than four kilometers away from home by herself. Why was the boundary set exactly at four kilometers?

She wanted to be like everyone else. She sang in the town choir, collected postage stamps, taught a beginners' course in Esperanto. One time, she even went to an Esperanto summer program.

"Don't forget your pills, Iris!"

"I won't forget them, Mama!

When it rained she would sit at home and make slides from her photographs, or take paper and pastels from the drawer and create little works of art. She kept up correspondence with a whole slew of pen pals and showed off the letters to her girlfriends, breathless from excitement that someone out *there* had sent a note to their small Bosnian town, where the air was thick with the smell of coal dust. The letter was a sign from another world.

When she was in good health, Iris scaled the town's nearby mountain, step by step, all the way to the top. This happened exactly once in her entire life. At the summit there was a little house for those who reached the top of the world.

"Iris, why are you overextending yourself like this?"

To be like the others. I wanted to go with them, to show them what I could do.

She lived to go beyond the limits of her illness.

The war came to Kakanj. Twice she had to flee into a bomb shelter. Only twice. And that is when death arrived. Iris tripped in the doorway at her friend's apartment and never got up again. Foam formed at the corners of her mouth.

"Iris!"

She was gone.

It rained at the funeral in Čatići.

Iris' aunt in Zagreb found out about her death only after the funeral. The message traveled a long way before it reached her. News will circle the globe before it finds the person it was meant for. It wasn't possible to call her directly from Kakanj. She wasn't able to go to the funeral.

Once she found out about her niece's passing, she took out an envelope and sent a donation to the address of the Esperantists: *in honor of Iris Tokić of Kakanj, who died at the age of 24.*

I folded up the aunt's letter and went over to the window. I stood there silently.

Two soldiers marched down the street. A couple of Pusses in Boots.

The war has sharpened their swords.

Backing up from the window, I collapsed on top of the papers on my desk.

I poured a cup of coffee down my throat. My coworkers were talking about the rape of little girls in Bosnia.

"And her mother was in the next room when she heard her daughter cry out, 'Mister, don't!'". My coworker was in the habit of repeating every horrific detail three times. At the second "Mister...!" I ran out of the room.

"Koka's coming this afternoon," said another coworker. Koka was a Bosnian woman, who was held for two months in the Omarska concentration camp near Prijedor, where Bosnian Serb forces had held non-Serbs. She was coming to tell her former classmate her story of survival.

The door opened soon thereafter. It wasn't Koka, but a man, who entered the office. "Do you remember me? I'm an Esperantist from Osijek. My nephew went with you to Norway once, to an Esperanto youth gathering." I remembered the man and his nephew, Joĉjo, too. Joĉjo and his friends played soccer at two in the morning at the North Pole.

Ten years have passed since then. Joĉjo no longer plays soccer.

Joĉjo's uncle wasn't a man who cried. Even when he had to spend several months in the hospital, he learned to enjoy himself. He bought a subscription for the hospital to *El Popola Ĉinio* as a surprise for his doctor, who had, once upon a time, learned Esperanto. It was his Christmas present for her.

Joĉjo's uncle was doing better now, but the latest news about his nephew had taken its toll on him. In my Esperantist circles, we'd lost touch with Joĉjo a few years after we got back from Norway. He was no longer interested in the language. Until his uncle told us that day, none of us had heard that Joĉjo went to work in the oil factory, that he married Snježana, or that he had two kids. When he was a boy, Joĉjo's parents went to work abroad, and so his uncle looked after him while he was still in diapers. His uncle bought him his first Esperanto textbook and found him his first Esperanto pen pal. He even bought him a special album to save all the letters.

"Can you take him on a trip somewhere where the boy will see how Esperanto works in the real world? I'll pay for everything. It can be anywhere, even to the North Pole!"

As it happened, I had been preparing to go to an Esperanto event in Tromsø, a city just above the Arctic Circle in Norway. The trip was on the expensive side, but Joĉjo's uncle didn't mind. His nephew should have everything his heart desires.

And now his uncle sat before me trembling. Joĉjo was a police officer when the war began. His wife saw him for the last time in August. He disappeared the second week of September in the village of Hrvatska Kostajnica. There'd been no sign of him since then. Not on the list of causalities, not on the list of captured, not on the list of wounded. Many had disappeared without a trace during the battles in the town that September. Joĉjo's wife was pregnant with their third child, due in January.

Joĉjo's uncle finished his update. We tried to give him courage. *Not everything is lost. There is still hope. Who knows?*

We grinded our teeth on those old, comforting clichés. The door opened. Koka had arrived. My coworkers surrounded her, she who had grazed death with her fingertips. Joĉjo's uncle stood up. He would send word if he found out anything. I accompanied him to the door and reminded him to let us know when Snježana gave birth. He smiled tiredly, assuring me that he wouldn't forget. If the baby's a boy, he said, they'll name him Joĉjo.

The phone rang. A friend wanted to know if we could give her any advice regarding her current predicament. She had been waiting for her citizenship papers for nine months already.

"Have a bit more patience. I'm sure your documents are lying on some bureaucrat's desk waiting for his supervisor's signature."

"And what if they deny my request for citizenship? More than six thousand people have been refused. And they don't have the right to appeal."

"Don't panic. We'll find a solution when you have a definitive answer. You haven't been denied just yet."

She sighed. "Anyway. How are you doing? Are you able to sleep at night?"

"Yes. Ever since I bought these wonderful dehumidifying plants, I'm able to fall asleep much more quickly."

"Ask the florist if he also sells plants for citizenship papers related anxiety."

I clumsily tried to lift her spirits. The new Croatian state confirmed citizenship for its residents through the *domovnica*, a formal certificate of citizenship. Whole swaths of the population suddenly found out that they didn't officially exist. Many of these people, it was true, had lived in Croatia for more than three decades, but that argument was not good enough. *Prove it! Where's your birth certificate? Where was your father in 1947?*

And so began the great document search. People went back to their native villages and wrote their forgotten relatives. It was worst of all for those who unexpectedly discovered that they'd been born abroad—in territories that were no longer part of the same country as Croatia. At two in the morning, these same people would grab a thermos of tea, a sandwich, and a sleeping bag, and spend the night outside the appropriate government agencies in order to apply for their papers. Without a certificate of citizenship, they couldn't get a passport. Without the *domovnica*, they couldn't buy a home—and there were many people all over the country who urgently needed to buy the homes in which they had been living for years. Many properties that had once been rent free, given out by employers or by the state, now needed to be privately owned.

Posters hung everywhere: *If You Can't Get Your Certificate of Citizenship, Call This Number for Help...*

Good advice was available... for a price...

Loud and lively, Koka began to tell her story.

"Start at the beginning!" said one of my coworkers excitedly.

"When Silvo, the president of the Croatian Democratic Union Party in Prijedor, was imprisoned in May, I knew that it was my turn to get arrested too. I was his vice-president after all. Every day I waited, expecting them to come and take me away. A whole month went by. Then, two men in uniforms appeared at my doorstep. They shoved me into a police car and took me to the station. I spent the night in a cell where another prisoner was already waiting. I recognized him as a well-known lawyer.

"'Good evening, friend!' I greeted him, happy to see a familiar face. Without a word, he put his finger to my lips. It was clear we were being listened to. I went quiet.

"Then they interrogated me. I knew all my interrogators by name. We all knew each other well. We all lived in the same town.

"The next day, they stuffed me back in the same car and took me to Omarska. At the entrance to the camp we were forced to empty our pockets and line up against the wall with our hands behind our heads. I managed to hold onto my purse between my knees.

"We were standing at the wall, when all of the sudden I was hit by a fit of laughter. It was one of those stupid situations where everyone reacts in their own strange ways. I started to convulse and cackle. Everyone in the nearby buildings thought I'd gone insane, that I'd 'broken'. 'Broken' in camp slang meant you'd left reality behind, began acting totally crazy.

"It bothered me that I'd been in their hands for two days and no one had bothered to check the contents of my purse.

"'Anyone want to see what's inside my purse? I've been walking around with it for two days already!' Someone came forward. He looked inside, but didn't take anything out."

"Were you raped?" blurted out one of my coworkers impatiently.

Koka took a cigarette out of her bag. "I started smoking again there. Yes, I was raped. But that's not the worst of it. Take a look here. Touch my ribs. Those two are broken. I'm amazed that there aren't any bruises on my chest. They beat mostly from the back."

"How'd you get out of there?"

"That was simple. When TV cameras came from abroad and discovered the concentration camp, the leaders decided to release all the women. There were twenty-eight of us. But it was really a prisoner-of-war camp. After the first few days there, I made a career for myself getting coffee for the camp commanders. The high point was when I was promoted to work in the kitchen. I'd earned the right to give out plates. No talking, just giving out plates. Afterwards, I found out that 11,000 people passed through the camp, but when I was in the kitchen every day for two months, more or less, there were never more than 2,886 plates. That was the highest number of plates that we ever gave out at one time from the kitchen.

"We had our tricks for counting the plates. We couldn't count out loud or make any marks, of course, but with the plates we were able to ascertain the number of people imprisoned in the camp at any given moment. And I saw enough dead bodies every day to fill up this room from here to the window." She pointed towards the opposite wall. We turned to see how the sunlight shined diagonally through windowpane.

"Could you bathe there? Could you change your clothes? What did the women do when they got their periods?"

"Well, in that sense the women's section of the camp was relatively well-equipped. The women's branch was headed by someone who had run a women's prison before. He knew what he was doing. We were even given strips of cotton for the two months I was there. When someone poured boiling water on my hand in the kitchen, I received clean gauze to make a bandage."

"Was that an accident?"

"There were no accidents there. At another point, they took me in for questioning. I got cramps and they had to take me out of the room. The dossier in front of the examiner was hugely thick, so I didn't suspect at all that it could have been mine. Later someone deigned to explain to me what I was accused of. I understood they'd made up some pretty big charges against me. I was accused of being a member of a separatist government for the region. Maybe Silvo blurted out I was a part of this imaginary organization when they threw him in prison. I didn't have many chances to get the details from him. I saw him in the concentration camp right before they murdered him. I heard his screams coming from the interrogation room after they'd put him in there angling for a confession. They let him suffer for ten days before he succumbed to the wounds he received from their beatings.

"But where was I? In a word, the concentration camp was the place you started to think like a real Ustaše. They let me and the other women go and I went back home to Prijedor. Soon after I got back, my acquaintance let me know that my name was on the list of those to be assassinated. As soon as the opportunity presented itself, I escaped to Croatia. Help came soon enough. Foreign aid workers in the country were taking caravans of people who wanted to emigrate from Bosnia. I announced myself at the Norwegian Embassy, where the whole affair was being arranged. It was enough to say that I was coming from Omarska and they transported me across the border.

"When we got to this side of the border, the Croatian soldiers put on quite the show, welcoming us with care and grace. One of them kissed the hand of the Red Cross functionary who was leading us around. They put me up in the Hotel Intercontinental. From there I called my relatives in Zagreb and told them I was here. I moved in with them and now I'm here in the city, looking for work. All's well that ends well. Look at this—today my relatives' dog jumped on me so happily that he tore my last pair of tights."

I looked closely at the tear on her knee. The mark of a pet's affection.

"I'm sorry I've taken up so much of your time. There's so much to tell. What time is it? Oh, already! I'll see you all later. Bye for now! I have a meeting with a women's organization. The directors visited me when I was still in the hotel and gave me a bottle of perfume. Perfume! They didn't ask whether or not I needed any underwear."

Koka buttoned up her jacket, covering up her mangled, recovering ribs, and left.

The streets of Zagreb carry thousands of similar stories, crisscrossing on the sidewalk. Not everyone is able to persevere as well as Koka.

The office was silent after Koka left. How to get back into the flow of things that her arrival had interrupted? The unexpected ringing of the phone helped.

It was the principal of a primary school on the line. He was letting us know that we had his permission to teach Esperanto in his school. In all honesty, he said, he had to fight for Esperanto a little bit because several of the teachers considered the language to be a vestige of communism, but now everything was in order. Forty students had expressed an interest in the course—two groups—and the school had agreed to pay the teacher. Students wouldn't be required to purchase their textbooks either. The school would cover all the costs.

I was excited to speak to the children about Esperanto. After all the hours that they had to spend in bomb shelters, after all the violence around them.

"The textbooks need to be corrected. Please don't distribute the books to the students before we've made the appropriate edits. We'll fix the mistakes here, in the school library."

"What do mean *corrected*? What's your goal here?" I asked skeptically.

"Well, the textbooks are a bit old-fashioned. We need to update them."

"Old-fashioned? Not that much. We printed them only a few years ago, for the hundredth anniversary of Esperanto in 1987."

In an instant, I understood what he meant when he spoke of "updating" the books. In 1987, the book had been published in Zagreb, Yugoslavia. In 1992, Zagreb was the capital of a newly independent Croatia. Our enemy Yugoslavia needed to be driven out from the pages of the textbook.

I had wished so strongly for the chance to give Zagreb two new Esperanto classes. I took a small bottle of whiteout, arranged the forty textbooks in front of me, and transformed the offending YU into a blank, white stain. The letters were obstinate. They refused to be erased. When I covered them with the white liquid, the paper bubbled and the letters swam to the backside of the page where they were still clearly legible. I considered the matter for a while and found a package of tiny stickers from Japan in a drawer, with which I could cover up the spots one after another. Where the YU could still be read there was now a cheerful little picture with the words: *Mia amas Esperanto-n!* I Love Esperanto! The accusative ending *-n* was set off from the rest of the word by a hyphen. Not on account of any offense, however.

I made a deal with myself that I would bring the books back to the principal's office the next day if I was again awoken by sparrows. So it was. The principal greeted me politely, sitting at his desk with a list in hand. Not a list of students, but of further corrections. He turned out to be quite pedantic. I had wiped out the name of our former country only in the publisher's address. The new list was much longer. He'd found that abhorrent word "Yugoslavia" four more times. We'd need to replace it with "Croatia".

I took the list from his hand and scanned it curiously. What else troubled him? He intended to cross out the word *komunisto* everywhere and change the translation of the Esperanto word *policisto* with the new, more current Croatian term *policajac* instead of the socialist-inspired *milicioner*. An even greater sin had been committed on page forty-four. There, an announcement listed the addresses of Esperanto clubs in each capital city of Yugoslavia's former republics. He could not allow for such an advertisement to be distributed in his school.

I gave him back the list. He put down his red pen, the one with which he corrected the world, and shook my hand. I exited through the school courtyard.

Another ordinary day fights to keep on going.

The song of sparrows wakes only the luckiest amongst us.

MAY IN SARAJEVO

Anyone who was young enough to belong to the World Esperanto Youth Organization in 1973 was at the congress that year in Sarajevo. The young Esperantists stormed the city that summer, each participant taking back with them their own distinct impression of the town. I was the congress secretary. Sarajevo had already welcomed me in May before the festivities began. Before that, I'd only known the city from poetry collections. Now I had the chance to get personally acquainted with those verses. At the train station, arches of water sprang from the lips of stone frogs and greeted me upon my arrival.

I spent my time at no. 8 Vase Pelagića bent over reams of official congress letterhead. It was violet, decorated with a stylized image of a bridge. The Esperantists shared their space with the office of the Czech minority community. In one of the cabinets, which even back then I regarded with a bit of nostalgia, there was a set of several small copper pots that the Czechs used to brew their coffee between meetings.

The Year 1973. *Then.*
The Year 1992. *Now.*

Bombs are falling on Sarajevo. As I type the city's name—a city I can call my own—its famed Hotel Europe is burning. The smoke rolls slowly, heavy and suffocating. Where is the smoke going? To the next street over where the congress offices used to be? Are former congress participants, back in their comfortable faraway countries, coughing as the smoke from the TV screen seeps into their living rooms? The stench of scorched memories spreads from Sarajevo out into the world.

Memories of the same city are preserved unspoiled in our Esperanto literary anthologies. Poul Thorsen forever fixed the city in our literature with his poem *Early Morning in Sarajevo*. Do you remember it the way he does?

Above the mosque sits a sliver of moon
Embracing a pale white star
Sharp as a scythe, it makes night from the noon
A reminder of Turkish wars

Spice-scented winds carry me off to bed
The flutes bring their song to an end
Night shyly wraps a dark veil 'round her head
Cicadas cry out their lament

Everyone is struggling to save their bits of memory. I, too, struggle.

The truth is my alarm clock fell in love with him first. The clock started it. It happened like this: It was late at night, after I'd already shut off the lamp. A beam of light from a passing car ran across the ceiling and then—silence. The only audible sound left in the room was the clock. She was an entirely ordinary, everyday sort of clock. And like all clocks, back in Croatia she had recited her usual refrain: *tick-tock, tick-tock.* That's how she spoke at home. Now, here in Sarajevo, she had changed her language. It was crystal clear, no doubt about it. She was now saying: *Kemal, Ke-mal, Ke-mal.* How amusing! My alarm clock had learned a foreign language and spoke it beautifully too. I was pleased with her progress. It didn't even occur to me to give the clock a good shake and set her back to her old way of talking. I giggled into my pillow and repeated after her: *Ke-mal, Ke-mal, Ke-mal.*

And so began the month of May in Sarajevo.

When I woke up in the morning, I no longer remembered the incident. The day had other surprises in store for me. But the alarm clock had not forgotten. She had an excellent memory. Moreover, it sounded like she'd been practicing the whole night. She spoke very fluently now: *Ke-mal, Ke-mal, Ke-mal...*

The new sound suited her very much.

The next morning I bumped into him— Kemal. I couldn't even look him in the eye. It was too embarrassing. It wasn't his eyes I was worried about, but mine. You could read the whole story right there, in my eyes. And in my alarm clock.

I looked down at his shoes and at his hands, but when I had to look up, my eyes went no higher than the collar of his red shirt. The top button was open and, looking through the buttonhole, I could see a small red thread. I was tempted to grab the thread and tear it off, but I resisted the urge.

When evening fell and it was time to go home from work, he announced that he had some free time. By sheer coincidence, I wasn't in any rush either.

"Where are you headed now?"
"Nowhere. You?"
"Same."

From ul. Jekovac, you could see the whole of Sarajevo and even a bit further out. He excitedly began explaining something or other about the city while I listened, rapt. Not that I could repeat a word he was saying. I was looking a little at Sarajevo and a little at him.

An ant was crawling on the table between us.

"Look out! They're listening!"

He burst out laughing again.

The ant was well trained and promptly retreated.

"Should we go back? Are you cold?"

"No," I lied and looked into his eyes. He knew I wasn't telling the truth. We both knew it.

The lovestruck are capable of anything. They can pass a test without studying. Save up just the right amount of pocket money. Cook up a delicious soup from two carrots and whatever else is lying around.

I was becoming more capable too. I could wake up at five in the morning and not feel the least bit tired the whole day long. Then, I memorized his phone number. All six digits. Me, who couldn't keep more than three numbers in my head at a time. Early in the day, I called him just to hear how he pronounced the r in *Good Morning*. At eleven, I called to ask how many hours were left until six o'clock. At three, I called to see what page he was on. At four-thirty, I wanted to know if he could come any sooner since it was too long to wait all the way until six. Soon I was getting jealous of Miki, the boy he was studying with.

The month of May looks different in Sarajevo. Say what you will, but this is the most beautiful city in the world. Tramlines that end in Ilidža. Benches full of people on Wilson's Promenade. Magical phrases all over the city that begin with the word "Kemal".

After that he left for far away. So far away that I couldn't even bear to call the place by its name.

Sarajevo changed without him. I presume that Ilidža is now a totally unremarkable place. I haven't been back there, but I can just imagine. I'll bet the grass there is so mediocre, you can't even lose your glasses in it. The place is surely swarming with gnats.

I sit and wait for the postman. And write long letters. Their recipient will learn from them the sad fact that the month of May doesn't last so long in Sarajevo.

All sorts of things have changed. You'll say I'm exaggerating, but sometimes late at night when everyone else in the building is asleep, I hear my alarm clock repeating his name.

Such was the story according to my congress diary in 1973.

Two decades later, Sarajevo is burning. The city's children, scrambling up cherry trees to taste the fruits of May, are shot and killed. In a world with many kinds of cherries, there are no others that taste as good as those you eat after coming out of a bomb shelter. The sunlight bursts with flavor; the air is nourishing and rich. Cherries are a gift from heaven, and to heaven they will send you.

My days now begin with the news from Sarajevo. The number of casualties, the number of wounded. Yesterday twenty-eight people were killed. I picture a classroom full of children, so as to better imagine the horror.

My imagination and good thoughts can also protect my friends. When I was last able to call them, the Esperanto office in Sarajevo had not yet been demolished. They weren't yet starving. How many months have passed since then?

My clock has gone silent. She's grown old since my student days. Alarm clocks nowadays are all electronic. They don't know the old language.

When the war ends, peace will come. Kemal will send a very clear message: I am alive and so is everyone that you love.

And when the trains are running again, we will meet. I'll tell him how I dreamt that his diploma from Beijing University was lost in a fire. He'll look at me as if to refute the nightmare and his eyes will be as naïve as they were at the time of the congress. I won't be able to read in them how much agony he has seen.

We'll eat grapes, remembering those we washed in the office in old Baščaršija. *Do you remember the sound of the water hitting the copper?*

That's when there will be peace and fruit will taste like fruit and not like death.

A HOME
IN PRIJEDOR

for Zeno Hudeček

The ersatz state of Yugoslavia was split apart by canons.

My girlfriend Judita's parents lived in the Bosnian city of Prijedor, where the majority of the residents were Muslim. Her parents themselves were Catholic Croats.

After the war began, the city fell under Serbian rule. From the Prijedor region, the world received the first hair-raising reports about the concentration camps in the villages of Omarska and Trnopolje, where thousands had perished.

For months, it was impossible to call her parents in Prijedor. Telephone lines had been cut between Croatia and any territories under Serbian rule. You could get in touch with those same regions from abroad, however. So Judita would call Paris and whisper a message into a friendly ear over there that she would want passed on to her parents. You could call Prijedor from Paris. You could also send a fax, assuming that the electricity wasn't out at that time and the city's one fax machine wasn't busy. And if the fax was received, you would have to get it all the way up to the tenth floor of an immense apartment building, where the elevators were no longer in working order.

There, far above the sorrow of the streets below, lived Judita's parents.

It was possible to emigrate from Prijedor, if the applicant had the necessary dozen or so certified official papers and agreed to sign a document promising never to return and renouncing all rights to one's possessions. Overloaded with over half a million refugees from ethnically Croat regions under invasion, Croatian authorities accepted Bosnian migrants only after a rigorous screening and preferred to let in only those who did not intend to stay in the country, but were rather headed elsewhere.

Judita's parents had been born in Croatia. Their children were born there and they owned property there. But the storms of life had planted them in Bosnia, and there they lived a quiet, slow-flowing life. A house in the village of Brezičani, not far from Prijedor, served as their family's holiday cottage. In the garden, onions grew under the soil.

Then the war came and sent tanks to till the flowerbeds.

While Judita and her siblings in Zagreb were busy collecting all the required documents to repatriate their parents to Croatia, their father Zeno fell down the stairs one night during a blackout. He sustained multiple fractures. The best-equipped hospital near the town was in the city of Banja Luka. All his many broken bones had to be set in immovable plaster casts.

The news got to Zagreb from Italy.

"Zeno fell down the stairs, broke a few limbs, and is wearing a cast."

"Do you know the details?"

The Italian messenger knew nothing more than that.

They had to call the world over to see if anyone might be able to reach Prijedor by phone. But they could get no other information other than the fact that he had been seen by a doctor in Banja Luka.

When all the documents for their parents' immigration were finally ready, they needed to be expedited to Prijedor. Without those documents in hand their parents would be neither able to leave Bosnia, nor able to enter Croatia. But how could the papers be sent without a functioning postal system?

The siblings decided to send the documents to their friends abroad and have them faxed to Prijedor. They stood in line at the local office of the Catholic aid agency Caritas Internationalis, handed over the documents, and hoped that they would reach their destination. They called a friend in Paris, who in turn called their mother, and told her to get to the Caritas branch in Prijedor where the documents would be waiting. Copies of the same documents were also faxed to each of the checkpoints along the border that were now under the control of peacekeeping soldiers from the United Nations.

And then the children waited. And waited. In agony.

The children knew well the story of how their father Zeno spent his youth. He was fourteen years old when the war—the previous war—began. The son of well-to-do parents, he studied at a good gymnasium. The first time the police searched his home, he was playing the piano. At the end of the Second World War, he was barely eighteen. The new regime in Yugoslavia sought to purify the city of its "decaying bourgeois elements." Zeno and his brother were arrested, the youngest prisoners in their crowded cell. At night, the door to the cell would open and someone's name would be called. He would never return. Shots rang out instead.

Among the captives, there was also a group of professors, who organized a study circle for the young people in the prison. Zeno's brother perfected his mathematics there, in a prison cell, under the watchful eye of a strict tutor. Zeno himself learned graphology from a former court-appointed specialist in handwriting analysis. Years later, whenever he was in good spirits, he would apply these skills to his friends' scribblings. In the cell, where Zeno spent a year and a half, he and the other prisoners staged entire plays to keep their minds busy and heal the wounds of their regular physical and psychological beatings.

Not a half-century has since passed. The horror has returned.

Before all else, the parents needed to get an exit visa from Serbian authorities. Then, they had to secure a space in the caravan of automobiles taking people out of Bosnia. How could their father fit into a car encased in his plaster shell? From Prijedor, the parents would have to pass first of all through a zone under the control of a battalion of Nepalese peacekeepers. After that, they would pass through the Jordanian-administered zone. There they would finally reach Croatia, at whose border their children would be waiting from them the entire day.

Paris sent word that their father was coming on Wednesday. Judita and her brother set out early that morning for Novska where the caravan was supposed to arrive. On the way, she fixed her gaze towards the horizon in the direction from which the convoy of refugees would come.

The message from Paris had been sufficiently precise: there was no more gasoline available for purchase in Prijedor. Father would have to be transported in the back of a hearse owned by a funeral parlor that still had a stock of fuel. Awaiting the hearse would be someone with a few canisters of gasoline, who would then pass these containers onto the driver in exchange for transporting their father. A father traded for some gasoline.

Judita made it to Novska. The great wait began.

A small Arabic sign hung from a building, the likely headquarters of the Jordanian battalion she surmised. She knocked on the door.

"Salaam!"

"Alaykum al-salaam!"

Peace be upon you. She knew how to greet them.

Then, silence. The conversation continued only haltingly. She had wanted to explain that she was waiting for her parents who were soon coming across the border. In a hearse. But the meagre bits of English that either side possessed were only enough to carry their discussion forward not more than a millimeter.

Tea was served. And then served again. Their inability to communicate only made them more nervous. Here was the great problem of the UN peacekeeping mission: soldiers engaging in the same tasks were unable to communicate with each other. The Jordanians and the Nepalese across the border had no way to understand one another.

Suddenly, the door opened. It was as though some good fairy somewhere had heard their wish and conjured a familiar face: an Arabic translator from Jordan who was an acquaintance of Judita's from her student days.

"Mohammed! Is that you? What are you doing here?"

"Translating. And you?"

"Waiting for my father."

The translator knew the rules. No one knew exactly when the caravan would arrive, but it wouldn't be necessary to check all their gas tanks when they came. When word came from the Nepalese zone that the caravan was approaching, they would ask to send the hearse ahead of the other vehicles and speed up their father's arrival to the other side.

An entire day of waiting.

Tea served yet again.

One soldier called another *bulbul*. Judita recognized the sounds from Prijedor, where in their Islam-inflected dialect they used the same word for "nightingale".

"Is that some sort of bird?" she asked.

Joy at the meeting of two words. Their approximate pronunciation had brought them together. The nightingale had left behind its Arabic pseudonym in a Bosnian garden during some Ottoman-era war.

Another glass of tea. This time in honor of the flight of the *bulbul*.

Night fell. The caravan was approaching, already very near according to the official announcement. Here was the first bus of refugees.

The tea drinkers surrounded the bus, rifles at the ready to protect the oncoming vehicles. From out of the bus came frightened women and sleep-deprived, teary-eyed children. Outside the air froze. There was no hearse. Their father would not arrive at the border that night.

Judita drove around until midnight, bringing women and children who had just arrived in the convoy from Bosnia to different addresses around Zagreb.

The next day, a note from Paris fell gently from her office fax machine: father is too weak to get into the car. Their friend Saša, who had successfully gotten in touch with Prijedor from the French capital and had put together the details of Judita's father's absence at the border, wrote out the message in her own outgoing, large-looped handwriting.

Silence.

Father is too weak to be transported across. He is lying in bed on the tenth floor of a building with neither electricity nor water.

Several days passed without any word.

The news came from someone in Italy: father had died. His funeral was last Tuesday. It was Thursday by the time the message came around.

Judita took her sons to the cemetery. The boys lit candles:

"For my grandfather."

"And for my grandfather too."

The flames flickered as the night grew dense.

Weeks passed.

The process repeated itself. Judita called her friends abroad, so they could let her mother know to hurry. She should give away everything she had to give, and just let Judita know when she'd secured a spot on the next bus.

But her mother wasn't so quick. It wasn't so simple to get rid of all the things she'd amassed over the past five decades.

She had to visit the government office and announce her intention to emigrate. She had to certify that she had given up the right to her property. And she looked everywhere for something to pack her few belongings into. There were few pieces of luggage left in the town. Cardboard boxes were nowhere to be found. Everyone had used them as firewood instead.

Judita's mother remembered that she had some plastic sheets in their cottage in the village and used that to pack up her things. First and foremost was Zeno's favorite mug, from which no one else was allowed to drink. Then, the copper kettle that the two of them used to brew a pot of coffee each afternoon, in typical Bosnian fashion.

A noise at the door. The new tenant, heavy with suitcases, was already moving into the next room. Mother spread out her large sheet of plastic and stared at the kitchen—the essence and spirit of decades past.

She went to the grave to say goodbye.

When she got back to her apartment, a second intruder was already moving in, arguing with the man who'd got there more quickly before him. Cursing and screaming. Mother collected the glasses from which her life had been drunk.

The next day, her friends and neighbors accompanied her to the bus. Greetings and whispers. *Tell him I say…* She'd pass on the message. She wouldn't forget. The local Esperanto teacher also approached the group of parting friends.

"And ask your daughter to please forgive me, if I've offended her in any way…"

Mother thanked them all for the fond farewell.

Would the last time she'd see Prijedor be through the window of a bus? There, high above it all, on the tenth floor, she'd lived her entire life.

Three hours later, in another country, her children embraced her. They remarked on how she'd lost sixteen kilograms in the past year.

She spoke slowly, with a Bosnian accent. The knots in her thoughts unraveled with difficulty.

They ran a bath for her as soon as they arrived at her children's place. She starred in awe and admiration as the hot water flowed and flowed.

That night, the grandsons fought over who got to sit next to their grandmother. She hugged them tight, trying to blot out the memory of seeing so many buildings on fire from her balcony. Rumor has it that they burned only the homes with "four-cornered roofs," made from four distinct trapezoidal parts. The building most beloved by the Muslims. Around the flames, would-be arsonists in uniform snickered and sneered in savage delight.

She shook her head to rid herself of the image and smiled, somewhat lost in thought. She stretched her arms towards the radiator.

How well it warmed her.

It would be a few days before the children would hear about Zeno's last fearful days. She couldn't speak about it right away.

It was only by coincidence that the city's atrocities hadn't yet reached the skyscraping apartment building in which they had lived. The building's residents were saved by their neighbor—a police officer—who threatened any armed visitors with his own pistol. "No reason to search this building! Everything's in order here! There aren't any guns here."

In peacetime, that neighbor—a policeman and an ethnic Serb—was often mocked for being a simpleton. Now, in the midst of war, when everything was the opposite of what it once was, his word suddenly took on the power of the highest authority. At least for a certain amount of time.

The mere fact that someone was searching his building for Croats, just as had happened when he was a teenager, threw Zeno into a deep depression. The story of his childhood all of a sudden began to replay itself. Here it was alive and well, and crueler than before.

"I'm not going anywhere! I will not flee," he said darkly when the rumor reached him that Croats and Muslims were being kicked out of other buildings and sent away.

The violence of his youth sealed his old age.

When he fell down the stairs, that was, in a sense, his escape, fleeing to where no persecutor could follow.

Trying to follow the conversation, his small grandson posed a question: "Why did he die? When we prayed for him was it so he would live or so he would die?"

AN UNMOBILIZED HAND TOWEL

for Pero Djaković

Five children in the kitchen.

"Mom's out at the bazaar. She'll be back soon. Please have a seat."

Summer was coming to a close. The air outside was heavy and suffocating, hinting with each passing day at the long and cruel winter ahead.

Fruit was best purchased now, an hour before the bazaar closed, when it was sold much more cheaply than earlier. Wasps buzzed around the sellers and pollenated their merchandise. Where a piece of fruit had split open, there the wasps were, greedily drinking up the summer.

August had left its bronze on the skin of sixteen-year-old Sana. She'd spent the holidays by the sea with her sister at their relatives' place. Two whole weeks.

A collection of polished stones next to a vase. A small wooden table in the shape of a tree trunk, waiting for the pot of soup that would come when the children's mother would return.

A noise from the floor, coming from a cardboard box. Apparently, there was some sort of animal inside. A ruffling of feathers.

"What's that?"

"A pigeon. We found him two days ago. Fell off the roof before it had even learned to eat. We're teaching him how to pick apart grains of wheat with his beak. Once he's learned that, we'll set him free. But for now, he's totally helpless against the cats. He doesn't know how to fly yet, the silly little thing! So we have to feed him. He doesn't understand that he needs to pick up the seeds with his beak."

A beginner's course in pigeon: First lesson! Hop to it! No mistakes!

"And your father? Is he still at work?"

"No, he has to go report to the army. Mom didn't tell you? He got a summons yesterday. We're not exactly sure what for."

"Report to the army? But he's a doctor!"

"A bunch of dads in the neighborhood got the same summons yesterday. We'd just gotten back from the sea and went to tell our friends that our dad got this letter in the mail. 'Mine too,' they all said. 'Mine too.' 'And mine too.' We don't know what it's all about. Maybe it's just to check in."

"Maybe. The war's coming to an end. There were talks in London just yesterday, and they're saying it looks hopeful. It's all here in the morning paper. Take a look!"

In the accompanying photograph, heads of state stood in elegant clothes, their faces twisted in stern expressions. The head of state from our country was shaking someone's hand.

The war is coming to an end very slowly.

When I was Sana's age, wars in history books were concluded with treaties. Peace marched at the head of every regiment. Soldiers came home with peace and took off their boots.

The current war, however, has hit us like an incurable plague. An endless number of agreements have been signed, and yet we hear every day about more bombs that have to fall, about more fathers who have to leave.

The rescued pigeon didn't even know how to pick up a kernel of corn with his beak.

A shadow slinked its way across the small maple tree growing underneath their window. Was it their mother back with her fruit basket?

A surprised shriek flew out of Sana's mouth:

"Dad!"

It was him. He was sporting a uniform that had never been worn before. It was still rigid, not wanting to conform to the contours of his body. He quickly threw off his boots. Each one had a buckle held down with two straps above the ankle.

"I've been drafted, mobilized," he greeted me. "You'll forgive me, but it's just too hot in this thing."

Mobilizi—to mobilize (v.) to call up, to prepare for war, ex.: to mobilize a division; to mobilize the troops, the reserves, the entire industrial complex. So it says in our great dictionary, the *Plena Ilustrita Vortaro*.

To mobilize a father. So says the military. The same military that just yesterday signed another peace treaty.

The youngest son put on the boots, covering up both his tiny little legs in their entirety. He brought the leather from one of them up to his nose and inhaled its freshly polished smell.

"It's so brand new!"

He was right. These boots were fresh from the factory. They'd not yet been implicated in anyone's murder.

The eldest son tried on the uniform's dress shirt. This time, the size was just right.

"Nice. I could wear this to school." The military look was all the rage.

The uniform was one of those you'd see in films about wars, where the wars happened on other continents. The fabric was covered in black-green spots, designed to camouflage the wearer among another continent's bushes. But these uniforms were to be worn by our fathers, and the bushes were the ones growing across our fields.

"Did they give you a rifle, Daddy? Will you serve in the Medical Corps, Daddy? Did they give you a handgun, Daddy? Maybe you got a Magnum?"

"What's a Magnum?" I asked them to clarify. I was unexperienced in matters of warfare. In my library, you couldn't find even one dictionary of military terminology.

Cousin Goran helped to enlighten me: a Magnum is an incredibly powerful handgun. It has an especially long barrel and can blow off whole body parts in a single shot. All this according to a little boy.

I came to understand that Goran was quite an expert when it came to firearms. The number of children I'd counted earlier was incorrect: there were not five, but seven children, in their family now. Two more had recently arrived from Slavonski Brod, a city that had for months been under constant bombardment. Goran and his sister had smoothly incorporated themselves into their cousins' family and even began to attend the local schools in their new city. It was too dangerous for them at home. *Brod* means "ship". *Slavonski Brod*—the ship of Slavonia, safely ashore on the banks of the river Sava. On the other side is the town of Bosanski Brod—the Bosnian ship. Before, the kids from Slavonski Brod would go to Bosanski Brod in the evenings to get ice cream. It was such a pleasure to walk across the bridge. Today, on the other side is a whole other country, one in which the war rages ferociously. The ship on our side was also under attack, filled to the brim with refugees.

"Does your daddy have a Magnum?" asked the smallest child.

"Not a Magnum. Just a simple handgun," said Goran with an air of authority in the riverside accent of his home region.

"And where does he keep it? On top of the radio?"

A very important question: where does Daddy put down his gun when he's resting? Because sometimes daddies and their handguns rest at home.

"Daddy, will you be on the frontline?" From a small mouth comes a big question.

Daddy doesn't know yet. He'll have all the details tomorrow.

"Daddy, are you allowed to wear your normal clothes now that you have a uniform?"

He is allowed, if he has the opportunity.

He buttoned up his civilian shirt quickly. He had to get back to the hospital and turn in his draft documents.

"How are you feeling about all this, Dad?" asked Sana. Her skin, browned by the seaside sunlight, had not yet paled at the news of her father's mobilization. The question ripened, ready to be answered.

"You know that this isn't my war. But at no time does the draft ask whether or not you want to go. A lot of bad things happen on the battlefield and I'm a doctor. I'll go wherever they send me and I'll help whoever needs me."

The father laced up his civilian shoes, his son untied his military boots. They felt too heavy. The full weight of their father's bit of wisdom was not yet fully felt. The pigeon, the beginner, stubbornly flapped its wings.

The next day, it was time to say goodbye. Every cheek presented itself for a kiss.

Mother had packed many suitcases in her time, but she had never packed for a war. She had forgotten to pack a hand towel.

Their father called the following day. From some hospital where he had taken a wounded soldier. He couldn't say where he was—the military has its rules for proper conduct. But you could smell the fire in his voice.

Of all the world's questions, the one about the hand towel was the quickest ever answered.

"Did you get the towel?"

"No."

The voice cut out from the receiver.

In my bathroom, warm water flows from the faucet. I dry my hands and stare at the hand towel. I remember the world in towels and cloths: Anna's hand towel covered with Italian lace. The towels from Gothenburg, heavy with gray softness. Sera's pieces of fabric embroidered with flowers. The large terrycloth squares at the Japanese hot spring that I could wrap around my entire body.

Memories of lost towels come back to me: a brown beach towel torn up by a storm on the island of Mljet. A white towel left out to dry on a hook in the Korean city of Busan. A rose-colored hand towel that I used to dab my sweat, left behind in a Chinese hotel.

I remembered expensive hand towels displayed in shop windows that caught my eye while strolling by. Saffron. Turquoise. The arabesque of Isfahan. Owners' names stitched intricately into the fabric. *Should it be sewn in with the same color or a contrasting shade?* The women selling the cloths tempting customers in voices sweet and smooth as honey.

The washcloths, towels, cloths of my memory mobilize and spread outward in all directions. Towels from well-off and comfortable countries, touched each morning by calm, contented hands.

Let those hands remember the ones who live without the luxury of hand towels.

Father will take the towel that is offered him and dry his hands. That feeling of cleanliness refreshes the soul like a whispered prayer.

Peace will return when their father will dry his hands and take a moment to look at the lasting cleanliness of his palms.

FATHER OF FIVE

A visitor from Japan was interviewing me:

"Have you lost anyone close to you?"

"No one. No one yet."

"Have any of your loved ones' homes been hit in the bombings?"

"No, not yet."

The "yet" didn't sound right, stylistically. It was too often repeated. It exposed an underlying desperation. The destruction had not yet ceased. What was true today could change by tomorrow.

The Japanese journalist had hardly reached the ground floor of my building when death made itself comfortable inside my phone.

A friend called. Her voice sounded confused.

"Is everything okay?"

"You haven't heard?"

A terrible piece of news was circulating around her village. About a father of five, who... she didn't know how to say it...

"Pero?! It can't be. He called home just yesterday."

The cuffs of my pants began to shake. My legs had accepted the truth before I could.

My tongue, convulsing in fear, rolled a crumb of hope around my mouth.

"He called yesterday and spoke with his eldest son. And he said that everything was fine, nothing to worry about. It's probably just a mistake. I'll speak with his family. How long ago did you hear about this?"

She had heard the news quite recently. Her friend had just phoned. The victim was still anonymous. A doctor had been killed, a father of five…

Our wishes always turn very selfish during a bombing. As soon you hear the bombs hissing near your building, the thought pops into your head: just don't hit *me*. Our hope offers our neighbors up to the bombs. Maybe death has found some other father of five, and not the one I call my friend.

I phoned the family. All five children sat in the kitchen. They did not sit alone. Death sat with them.

"What happened, Val?"

"It's awful. Father's been killed."

The eldest son was given the task of sharing news of the death with all those who called. Although each caller took a piece of that death with them, the home was still overflowing with it.

"How do you know? Who told you?"

"They came from the army. A few men from his battalion."

The heavy hand that had given them the news squeezed my shoulder.

"Should I come over?"

"No, Mother says that won't be necessary. The house is already full…"

On the other end of the call, I could hear his sister's sobbing.

I put down the receiver. The little girl's sobs filled my room. I sat down, shackled to the chair by those tears and waited to see whether I would turn to stone. I could move my arms, my hands, my fingers, my feet. Only my mouth stayed shut, the words stuck inside.

His daughter, Petra, had visited our office earlier that same day. The child of Esperantists, she hesitated by the door. "Do I need to introduce myself? I'm the daughter of…"

My coworkers looked at her admiringly. She used to come to our Puppet Theatre Festival every year and applaud the wolves and sheep. And now here she was, suddenly a teenager, her blond hair tied back with a ribbon.

"How you've grown this summer! Could you try on those shoes there? Try them on. That pair's an extra." During wartime, someone's always just received a package. That morning, a box of shoes had arrived. Petra liked the look of them. She took off her shoes and tried on the new ones.

"Too bad. They're too small, unfortunately."

She put the shoes back carefully, throwing them a longing glance. They were beautiful. Black, decorated with bits of gold.

And now they would have to dress all in black. Black—the color of sorrow.

"And your father?"

"He called us yesterday. Even told us where he was. He'd never been able to tell us that before. He calmed our nerves and told us not to be afraid, told us that he's doing okay."

"And the hand towel? Was he able to figure something out?"

"Yes, he got one. My uncle in Slavonski Brod was able to get him a towel."

"Well, what's important is that he has a towel at all," we joked.

But by that time, death had already wiped its hands on his washcloth. Death had already chosen him when he announced that he had been drafted, when his little boy was trying to put on his boots.

Death was watching him when he said that this wasn't his war. It stared at him when his eldest son put on his dress shirt and looked at himself in the mirror. Death had already made its decision as they sat there drinking juice in their summer-filled kitchen.

At what hour did death reach its decision? And how was its sentence carried out? By bullet? By handgun? By grenade? What was the last plant he saw?

I could see his dead blue eyes. I shut his eyelids in my mind. My fingers grazed his beard. A beard with many gray hairs; he had been approaching his forty-fourth year.

I'd first met him at the Esperanto Student Club. He was studying medicine. His future fatherly seriousness wasn't yet on display. On New Year's Eve, Vesna giddily gossiped away all his most embarrassing secrets: he, the son of a university professor, was loath to bathe. When they'd remind him that it was time to take a bath, he go to the bathroom, let the water run, and, sitting on the outside edge of the tub, get absorbed in a good book. After a few pages, he'd pull the drain and return to his family refreshed.

I envied his ability to play such tricks. I didn't have the courage to lie like that. I was afraid of being discovered for even lesser everyday offenses.

The young woman he fell in love with at the club was a very specific type. She kept her hair twisted in a braid, enviably thick and lovely.

I joined their club when I was still a beginner at the level of *leono estas besto*. Instead of *salono*—salon—, I'd say *salo*—salt. I was coming from the provinces. I didn't know how to curse and I would blush at every joke. The two of them had already finished studying *La tagiĝo*, used words like *elvagoniĝi*, participated in two congresses, and were already plotting a revolt against the older generation, who was ruining everything. They'd already seen the Cap of the North (whether in person or just on a map, I still don't know), ate lunch at Torben's place, and bought a copy of *The Kalevala* in Finland. I didn't know the first thing about *The Kalevala* and mixed up Urho Kekkonen with Julius Nyerere. The club only gradually accepted me. She gave me a haircut herself, in part so I could save a bit of spending money, but also so she could show me that my nose wasn't nearly as long as I thought it was.

I bumped into Pero on the tram and told him animatedly and expansively about how I'd lost the key to my dormitory the day before. And how I still couldn't find it when my friends had to leave to catch the last bus later that same night. Afraid that they'd miss the last bus, the guests threw themselves one after another over the window sill, careening into the garden below. Then, as soon as the last person hit the grass, I suddenly found the key.

Pero laughed at my misadventure.

"And what's new with you?" I ask condescendingly.

"I graduated yesterday."

He muttered like someone confessing that he had nothing interesting to share. Not like me, whose friends flew out the window last night.

I kissed him on tram no. 4, as befits all such auspicious occasions.

Immediately thereafter, he was called up for mandatory military service.

Back then, serving in the army wasn't something that made the marrow in your bones run cold. It meant time lost to endless tedium, to discomfort and deadly boredom. The worst was having to obey those brutes and listen to their lectures on things that no one actually believed in. To be a soldier back then had nothing to do with death or killing.

Several of us from the club went with him to the train station. His destination was Novi Sad.

When the train started to move, she broke off from the group and kept walking beside the train. They held each other's hands. As the train began to speed up, she started to lag behind. They touched fingertips, then only fingernails. Between their nails lay the whole of Yugoslavia. The country was held together by the mail in those days, letters written with warmth and love. The next time she cut my hair, I could feel the love in her fingertips, fumbling about at the back of my neck.

His return trip passed through the city of Zadar. After all the gray uniforms, the sea seemed so bright that he had to close his eyes just to look at it. One island, known before only as a frequent answer to clues in crossword puzzles, was especially enchanting. It was called Veli Iž, and it was there that he decided to live like Robinson Crusoe. She left the job that had been the center of her universe and became a housewife on the faraway isle. The whole world was reduced to him and the sea. From May to October they sat on the beach and looked out at the water. From that came five children, one after another, rocked gently to sleep in the cradle: *Val* for the waves, *Sana* for the river, *Petra* for the stones, *Dan* for the day, *Gaj* for the grove.

Seduced by letters smelling of Mediterranean spinach and olive oil, we on the mainland would go see them on the island. There we marveled at the creations of Čedo the carpenter, who had made furniture out of their dreams.

Nature flourished under their windows and in their rooms. They knew each of the sheep by name, from whose wool they made their rugs. They knew all the twists and turns of the fir branches that extended into their cupboards as though they were the shelves themselves.

The children took their first steps on the beach, from conch shell to conch shell. One winter, the winds began to howl and whirl around the island. They suddenly remembered how the theaters looked, all lit up for a premiere. An unfamiliar longing had awoken inside them. Dutifully, Pero sailed to his patients in a little row boat. The burden of the island's elderly rested heavily on his shoulders. The idea of return matured slowly in their minds.

After visiting his last patient, Pero rowed ashore. The wrinkles in the water smoothed swiftly behind him.

A wisteria took root in his new garden. I had given them the small seedling from my hometown. The plant felt much better in their care than it did in mine. It bore hefty flowers that called one out to touch them, just like the braids in her hair once did.

Beneath the plant was a handmade doghouse. Fish swam in an aquarium. On the wall hung three glass containers filled with three different sorts of sand that he had brought from the Sahara in his backpack. For his birthday, an occasion for which I regularly forgot to send him my wishes, he had wanted a map of China. A map of the solar system was already hanging on their wall. I was never brave enough to look and see: where are we in the cosmos?

Cicadas sing, sitting on tree stumps and bathing in the sun.
Their trochees stifled by resounding, bold iambs.
Noontime. Water spilling into silence.
A sun-soaked dithyramb.

So read his translation of a Croatian poem into Esperanto, the brightest verse in our anthology of *Kroatia Poezio*. The flow of my reading was stopped by the scene's everlasting imagery.

An ethnographic museum collection began to take shape on their walls. For every handcrafted village spindle hanging there they could tell long and complicated stories, in which the women who once held them came back to life. Even when none of the five children were practicing piano, the house was never silent: from the spindles and ancient hope chests, the tin plates and jugs, from antique clothes irons, and the old scissors used to shear sheep in days gone by, the sounds of our ancestors reverberated in their home.

I drank brandy from a glass engraved with the image of a dog's head. And as I held the glass, I felt as though I had known the dog personally since I was a little girl.

Pero was a great fan of the artist Ana Hutinec's sculptures. Her bulls, powerful and muscular, took up residence in their home. The bull flexed his muscles, never wanting to relax.

As a sculptor, Hutinec often worked on the image of the widow: old village women, silent and tearless, beaten by the whip of fate. Mute, they stand dressed in black and hopelessness. Pressed against their bodies, their hands are clasped tight, clutching a shining speck of something white: a thread, from which they will crochet something new. The white shred of fabric would be the only bit of color in the entire sculpture.

When I entered the home, there was no white thread at her breast. The plants in the garden were in full bloom. He had known each plant's name, each one's relationships and family ties, each one's likes and dislikes. Apples hung from the tree that he had trimmed. They would ripen by next month.

Petra was lying immobile on her bed, so as not to let the full weight of the pain press upon her. Instead the pain spread all over her pillow, from where no one could wash out the stain. Gaj and Dan stood like two stone statues, eyes darting from side to side. Sana was like a fairy exiled from the kingdom of youth. Val had grown old overnight. He shook my hand like his father would have. A candle burned in the kitchen. Its flame flickered.

At their home were a few men from his battalion, who had shared with him his less than two weeks of war. They imparted the details.

Someone came and announced that they'd found several wounded soldiers. The doctor gulped down his coffee and stood up. "Let's go, boys."

Where was he sitting in the ambulance? Who sat next to him? Where were the shots coming from? Was he killed before the ambulance caught fire? Who survived?

Questions posed in order to reconstruct the event. Death had its hour, its place, its manner.

"And what happened to the wounded soldiers he had gone to help?" she asked soberly.

I stood by the window and looked out at the garden. The delicate plant before me was covered in white buds. They would open soon.

"And how did they tow away the wreckage?"

Her imagination glued together all the details.

"With a tank."

That last word cut off the flow of questions. Through the windowpanes, the white-flowered plant heard nothing.

How could I help in this place of helplessness?

I volunteered to go stand in line and collect the necessary paperwork.

The army would take care of the funeral. I would have to get the death certificate at the Medical Tribunal, the government body which dealt with all fallen combatants. Second floor. Going through the front door, my curious and exceptionally indiscreet gaze, at least for a military setting, landed right on a window into the basement: a collection of black plastic sacks lined up one after the other. A thick plastic of a slightly higher quality than the bags you use to take the garbage out. Hanging near each sack was a small sign. Names, most likely.

Everyone in the sacks had his or her family waiting in the hallway. We were number eleven in the line that morning. It all worked very slowly. A young wife fainted right in front of us. The director of the Tribunal, his hair greasy from sweat and anxiety, extended his hand and offered us his condolences. He wasn't anxious without reason: someone there was refusing to identify their loved one's body. Although the corpse was in no way disfigured, the relative calmly observed, there was just no way that this was his brother. There was a distinct lack of co-operation between this relative and the authorities. The man asserted that the corpse was not his brother. Understandably, when his brother was alive, he looked absolutely nothing like the deathly face of this cadaver.

Everything came to a halt. The rest of us retired to the hallway and let the director resolve the case. Another woman fainted in the hallway. She was wearing a new black outfit. Black was the most fashionable color that summer. Sorrow itself.

Pero's sister stopped in the hallway and looked at the garden. There were grasses growing there, but she looked past them, and peered towards the emptiness above. I wiped my sweaty palms, pleased that neither of us had fainted. I paced from door to door. One was slightly open. On the other side were two women in long white lab coats, each analyzing something under a microscope.

Finally, our turn came. The two women who had fainted were revived, the unbelieving brother persuaded by some documents.

We sat across from the greasy-haired man. My eyes peeked over at the new state insignia. It was fresh, as though just pulled from the forge. Yet so many sacks have already been lined up in its honor. The flowers that decorated it seemed to be made of plastic. An unfamiliar guilty feeling forced me to look away.

The director opened up dossier no. 332 of the year 1992. *Last Name, First Name, Profession*: doctor. The folder had yellowed, as though the deceased had passed away long ago and we were researching something quite distant. *Location of Death*: he noted a geographic area far larger than would fit into the truth. I felt ashamed for him and looked down at my lap.

"*Number of Children:* four"

"Five," we corrected him in one voice.

A feeling of hatred flashed within me as we triumphantly corrected his mistake. I repressed the emotion, seeing that he was embarrassed. The draft had not called up the father of five, but the doctor living in such-and-such house on such-and-such a street.

"We won't be able to show you the deceased's body since he was so badly burned," he uttered this phrase quickly. He'd already said it many times that day. We had already known that fact, and nodded courteously in silence. Cooperation.

"Can we have the ring?" asked his sister, coolly and bravely.

The director picked up the receiver and ordered his subordinates in the basement verify whether or not they had a ring for the person in question.

Evidently, no one liked to do their job down there in the basement. "Please verify whether or not we have the ring. That's an order. His family is here. Call back immediately."

We continued with the paperwork. We came to the space for *Manner of Death*.

"Automobile explosion," he proposed. We accepted.

We once again went over the details that the soldiers had already told us: someone came in and informed them that in a particular direction were several wounded soldiers. The doctor promptly got into the ambulance and they started to drive. He sat behind the driver, next to his assistant.

They were ambushed. Shots were fired. Hit in the shoulder, the driver yelled out: "Doctor, get out!"

He turned to see that the doctor was already dead in his chair, covered in multiple shot wounds. Only his assistant had had the time to jump out. The doctor's body had shielded them from the bullets—only the assistant's backpack had been hit. As the survivors crawled out of the bullet-ridden ambulance, a rocket hit the gas tank and set the car ablaze.

"And how did they tow away the wreckage?"

"With a tank."

At the word "tank," the white camellias bloomed in my memory.

Silence.

No response from the basement. Incensed that this too was taking so long, the director called again.

"I ordered that someone check on the ring!"

"The ring is not here, Sir."

We felt unburdened.

The last space on the form was for a signature.

The funeral would take place Saturday at three o'clock. At the army's expense. The deceased's wife will pick a plot in the cemetery.

We nodded again and again, pressed down by our suffering.

The director extended his hand. *Please accept our deepest condolences.* Two women next to him picked up the dossier and filed it away.

Out to Lunch.

We were the last case that morning.

In the hallway, I recognized a young woman.

"Dunja, is that you?"

"Yes, it's me."

I knew her from the Esperanto Center. How many classes did she take before she decided to volunteer for the army?

"Can I ask you something? Do you have any influence over what happens at funerals? For the doctor, the father of five, could we do without all the coats of arms and patriotic slogans? He was a person of a different sort."

Dunja was sympathetic, but the funeral of a fallen soldier has its particular rituals: the flag on the coffin, military gunfire salutes, a coat of arms made from floral burial wreaths. Dunja listed all the routine elements. She had organized many such military funerals.

"Perhaps we could shorten the official part of the ceremony then?" I said humbly.

"You can write the eulogy and I'll read it out in the name of the army. I'll gladly accept any of the family's suggestions."

The negotiations were settled rapidly. The army would supply the coat of arms, the salutes, and the wreath. I'd supply the words.

Dunja brought us to another office where death announcements were prepared for the newspapers.

The receptionist looked over the text his wife had prepared and grimaced unhappily. Too many irregularities. How can we fit this into our rubric?

True enough. The death announcement that his wife prepared did have an unusual message. *We forgive everyone. You must also learn to forgive.*

The single-line invitation for forgiveness was longer than a whole newspaper page. It was directed at the men who started the war, at the men who made guns, at the men who profited from their sale. At him, who signed his draft papers, and at him, whose bullets hit the ambulance.

No wonder that the newspaper's usual stock of clichés did not suffice.

At night, I lay in bed thinking about the eulogy.

My grief would not let me fall asleep. I got out of bed and went looking for a poem that he had translated. There I found a line that I had never seen before:

And your green will never turn to autumn gold.

The empty side of the marital bed lay open like an abyss, larger than the void in the map of the stars. The abyss filled each child's room in a different way. It reached my home until I, terrified by its immensity, turned on the lights in my room in the middle of the night.

Despair in competition with forgiveness.

The consoling thought that the white flowers under his window would bloom again caused me only pain.

INTERMENT

She asked that we not buy any traditional floral wreaths.

Instead, each of us carried a flower plucked from our own personal gardens. Small and modest, and delicately held in our sweating hands.

Early September in the village cemetery.

It had been a long time since we'd seen each other in such great numbers. Friends traveled from Hamburg and Paris and saw themselves reflected in the deep pools of others' tear-filled eyes.

These people could make a strong case for the intellectual significance of Esperanto. Behind each one snaked a long, personal path lived in and for the language. We gathered together at this farewell and contemplated one another: who will be the next one that war will tear from our incoherent world? Mars the God had been quite discriminating this time—he selected one of the most high-quality individuals among us.

The family was standing in the mausoleum. Five children around their mother. The guests entered and mumbled words of condolence, trying in vain to sound soothing.

Draped with the national flag, the coffin stood surrounded by men from his battalion. The man who had driven him to the telephone, where he made his last call home. The man who had run to get him his last morning coffee before he took off in search of the wounded. And the man who had talked with him for a long time the night before he was killed.

One soldier held up a floral display in the shape of the national coat of arms with both hands. It was hot outside and he was sweating. His colleague came to replace him. Both of them were wearing uniforms with the same boots that his little son had tried to put on two weeks prior.

A choir of eight men was singing. The deceased would have appreciated the songs, if he could have heard them. I had started using the past tense while putting together the eulogy for Pero, hesitating before every verb. My love for him liked the present and only begrudgingly ceded him to the past. Each use of the past tense made another small cut.

There were four military burials that afternoon, all for soldiers from the same battlefield. In the neighboring chambers of the mausoleum, I recognized people who had fainted back at the office for fallen combatants. There we had hardly confronted death. And now was time for the interment of our loved ones' remains. *In-ter-ment*—to put into the earth—is a very powerful word, etymologically speaking. With it, we lay our most beloved people deep down into the earth. And scatter handfuls of earth above so as to enclose them in the soil.

The priests spoke without the usual platitudes, having known the deceased far better than a simple parishioner. The microphone carried their voices throughout the cemetery. Nearby, very near in fact, the garden that he had planted was still growing, its wisteria tightly embracing the porch roof.

The army bid him farewell with my text. Dunja hadn't changed even a single comma. I stood in the crowd and saw how my memories of him came forth from a mouth perched above the blouse of a soldier's uniform. I couldn't say anything about his condemnation of the war, not wanting to embarrass the person who would speak in the name of the armed forces. But I could not neglect to mention that we were burying a person who always had the audacity to speak the truth, even when it wasn't in his best interests. We in the audience knew how apt this description was. More than once we had been afraid he might lose his job, as he loudly complained that the new, patriotic government was sowing the seeds of intolerance. He came into conflict more than once with colleagues and bosses at the hospital about these very same issues. When he was called up to the front, we were afraid, not only because the war itself was dangerous, but also because he was not capable of keeping silent about his political beliefs. How could his conviction that violence was never the answer find common ground with the army's basic principle that warfare was the only solution?

The call to war was for him a test of his loyalty to the medical profession. He didn't hesitate. A war is full of victims, and they were asking for his help. Someone else in his place might have mentioned to the draft board that he was the father and caregiver of five children. He didn't bring it up.

Did he have occasion to fight for and defend the truth, in which he so believed? Death found him on the eleventh day after he left home. On the fifteenth day, or so it was said, a chance to rest would come, the right to return home.

The chance to rest had come. But it would be eternal.

Suddenly his wife stood up from among the relatives, holding a sheet of paper. She wanted to say something. The wind lifted her black veil. The crowd focused in on the pale visage before them.

"I am writing this to you by candlelight. It is the night before the funeral. I am writing to you by the light of my husband. This is not customary, but it is important. My stepping forward is not to make you cry or touch your heart. It is to plant a seed of human compassion. Everyone says that we must be strong. We will be strong. Others have warned that the pain will come later. I say, God willing, let it come! It is not easy to enter the kingdom of heaven. And if this loss is the straits through which we will enter, then we must thank the Creator and Ruler of the Universe for he has foreseen the means by which we will sustain ourselves as we march forward.

"Our family is not in ruins. Pero laid a solid foundation for us to build our home together. We will endure, those of us who are still on this side. Pero has left us with more than enough construction material.

"Find sustenance in Pero's light, those of you who can see well by it. As a woman, I speak to the women, the sisters, and the daughters here. Men and their wars swing together on a hanging leaf—will it fall or won't it fall? In his memory, I beg you to be patient and servile with your men—maybe what I say will come as a shock—but be humble and accommodating, and be in love with your husbands, your brothers, your neighbors, and friends. Today two, five, twenty of them will be killed. Tomorrow the same. War is terrible. Nothing is more important than harmony, love, and selflessness. Nothing can take precedence. If you are yet not capable of doing this, then pray that the Almighty will give you the strength to do so. I have been praying for months already together with my children that hatred should not flood our hearts.

"Friends, relatives, neighbors, colleagues—now is the time to end this hatred. It doesn't matter who started it or how many times it has happened. Our disputes are but petty things. I am not angry with anyone that my husband has been killed. We will not go on like this any longer! On the remains of my husband, I beg you to forgive and forget all unpaid debts. Let us move forward. We shall not allow our children and grandchildren to go to battle once again. But it depends on us. Let it be us, who begin the peace, about which everyone is talking. Let it be us, who cast aside all our calculations of who owes what and the invoices yet to be paid. Let us forgive ourselves, so that we might receive forgiveness. Only then can we once again live side by side with those who murdered our loved ones, or with those whose loved ones' blood is on our hands. This peace is the peace of Heaven. This is the message of my husband's life and the message of his death."

I looked at her hands as she folded up the paper and sat back down. One woman next to me broke out in sudden and genuine applause, then suddenly remembering we were at a funeral, guiltily put down her hands.

Enveloped by the warmth of the message, we walked more easily to the tomb. There, in the rocky soil was the grave.

By the grave stood his two daughters holding long-stemmed flowers and staring at the sandy soil as it slowly covered the coffin.

The line of those paying their respects was long. At the head of the honor guard, the soldiers fired off their farewell salute. The fatherland give its thanks with gunfire to all those who sacrifice their lives upon its altar. Happy is the country whose men need not be sent off with these salutes. For a moment, flames, like small clouds of yellow smoke, hung at the end of each rifle.

I watched the scene unfold as though it were a film. The bitterness in my heart gave up its place to forgiveness. Around me, people wearing faces distorted by war smiled good-naturedly. The wife's parting request lit a candle of hope in all of us.

That afternoon it seemed like the world's definitive peace treaty had been signed. We left the cemetery, feeling privileged to have participated in its official proclamation.

AFTERWORD MARS, OR THE DEVIL IN CROATIA

In the 1990s, the eastern half of Europe trembled, bringing into the homes of television audiences news of a cluster of peoples, ethnic groups whose names had rarely merited a mention on the world stage. These names were more likely to be found in linguistic atlases or in the pages of *Etnismo*. In many parts of the world, these names sounded strange, as though torn at random from old history books, as unknown as the Dacians or ancient Assyrians.

The nightly news troubled its spectators. After removing the word "socialist" from their countries' formal designations, dethroning busts of Lenin, and tearing red stars from their flags, the peoples of Eastern Europe, having lived so long under the pseudonyms of grand ideologies, unfurled their forgotten banners. They began to wave their old flags and update their old political slogans, searching eagerly for an identity. Who was to blame that for so many decades, so many centuries, they weren't able to live that identity in all its fullness? It was immediately clear. Looking around, it seemed to everyone that his neighbor was the arch-enemy. Our neighbors were the reason we were now living on foreign territory.

The flames of hatred hungrily consumed their kindling.

On television, we saw the president of the neighboring republic at some ceremony issuing a threat: *And if it can't be done by any other means, then it will be done by force of arms!*

At the words "force of arms"—a term that was used under the communists to talk about the fight against fascism or in newspaper crime reports—he turned his head sideways so the microphone wouldn't pick him up at full volume. Yet everyone still heard the threat. Military force quickly became the sole instrument of justice. But many conflicting interpretations of this same justice soon appeared and among them no compromise could be found. One or the other.

Yugoslavia was the name of the country to which I had belonged. They called it Mediterranean, Southeast European, Balkan. Balkan—the word comes from the mountain range that begins in Bulgaria, metaphorically used to talk about degeneration. Croatia was the name of one of the six republics of Yugoslavia, the one that was the most my own. *Hrvatska*, as the Croats call it. And Croatian was the language in which I was educated.

When I, a village girl studying at a city school, copied the class schedule out on the board for the first time, I abbreviated the names of our subjects: *mat.* for mathematics, *geogr.* for geography, *hist.* for history, *hrv. — Hrvatski —* for Croatian. Scribbling quickly, *hrv.* suddenly became *krv. Krv*—the Croatian word for blood. Hurriedly I erased the accidental allusion, wanting to keep the language pure.

Officially, the word "Croatian" was not especially welcome in post-World War II Yugoslavia. Related to Serbian, the language carried a malleable, many-sided name: Serbo-Croatian and Croato-Serbian, Croatian or Serbian, Serbian or Croatian. The idea changed depending on the compound's initial word. In practice, in our small corner of the globe, the language was called Croatian. In official parlance, however, the word "Croatian" reeked of ethnic chauvinism, the kind that subverted the underlying unity of Yugoslavia. In that word, all the misfortunes of the Second World War were preserved, that sad period in history when Croatia was the so-called Independent State of Croatia, a collaborator with fascist Germany.

As a child, the word "Croatia" was seen, first and foremost, on the side of the factory where batteries were made and in the name of the local social insurance office. There was also *Croatiatrans*, whose many buses crisscrossed the territory of Croatia and beyond. When I first learned Esperanto, the meaning of the word *trans*—across—was clear and understandable, thanks to those buses.

The etymology of the word "Croatia," on the other hand, has never been conclusively determined. Now, after so many massacres, the realization that *Hrvat*—Croat—rhymes with *rat*—war—is pounding at the door. It's the same with the word for brother. War *rat,* brother *brat.* In Yugoslavia, the state ideology taught us that all its peoples were brothers. Our brothers and our wars. We've had our fill of both.

Mars, God of Croatia is one of the classics of Croatian-language literature. It first appeared in 1922, written by the Croatian writer Miroslav Krleža. The phrase "Croatian writer" usually refers to someone born in Croatia, working in the Croatian language. Yugoslav writers were those with significance for the entire country, those whose influence reached beyond the borders of our republic. Krleža belongs to those of this second sort.

Mars was the god of war in Rome, a god of the Ancients. Our Croatian Mars marched through the literary landscape after the First World War. He found the countryside much to his liking. He's returned from the pages of novels and from history since then, and not only for the Second World War. Half a century later, better equipped and restored from his decades' long rest, Mars our God once again strikes his heroic pose. The end of the twentieth century does not like heroes. Mars the God has become the Devil.

Our main enemies in this war are called Serbs, the neighboring people. Together with several other Southern Slavic peoples, we formed the state of Yugoslavia after the First World War. Croats recognize Serbs (and vice versa) as soon as they meet: by their names, by the accents in their related languages, by their choice of words. For foreigners, it takes a long time to notice these distinctions. Serbs write their language in the Cyrillic alphabet, Croats with Latin characters. Both peoples are Christian: Serbs are Eastern Orthodox, Croats are Catholic.

After the 1991 referenda that resulted in the independence of the western republics Slovenia and Croatia, we had to draw more thickly those thin little lines that previously separated our spaces within Yugoslavia. The lines became the borders between new sovereign states. In the west, they hurriedly built customs houses and border stations. In the east, just as quick, they built war.

Why war? This small book does not pretend to have the answers. It only endeavors to preserve the feelings of the ordinary people, those of us who found ourselves like grass growing underneath it all.

The first time I arrived at the Slovene border—a place I'd passed through before unware and where now the engine stops and a border guard politely asks his questions—I was overcome by the feeling of separation. Family members, long having lived under one roof, suddenly got their own places. Many were overjoyed that it finally happened. I belonged to the minority that felt the bitterness of partition. The sense of amputation. In my life, I've had to say goodbye with a heavy heart to my classmates, roommates, lovers, co-workers. The time had come to say goodbye to my country, to redefine my identity.

Through the storms of history, great empires have fallen. Did their citizens have similar feelings?

Croatia's new map looks like an apple core, its body ripped apart by the teeth of neighboring peoples through the centuries. So was the interpretation of those predisposed in the country's favor.

Croatia looks like an open jaw, barring its teeth anew. It's looking for something to swallow. So it seemed from the other side.

There are marriages that end with a farewell dinner.

There are marriages that end in murder.

In my part of the world, neighbors who have lived together for seventy years are engaging in divorce by war. The First Serbo-Croatian War. The sound of it is frightening. After the first, there will be others.

"But Teacher, he started it!" the little boy defends himself. I hated that phrase from an early age, hearing it so often around the school yard.

The eternal accusation: the other one did it first.

This time, boys who started it, started brutally.

The world has already printed multiple editions of William Auld's epic anti-war poem *La Infana Raso*. When I was a beginner in Esperanto, we read *An Appeal to the Diplomats*, Zamenhof's famous 1915 call for peace. It sounded quaint, antiquated, irrelevant. Now that I'm a beginner at war, I've taken another look at the text. I'm startled, hit hard by how immediate it now reads.

I've been reading it in the bathroom, a room without windows. The mandated blackout: planes from Serbia fly over my city, illuminating their targets. So, I've hung thick curtains over all the windows to keep the light in. The windowpanes are covered with strips of tape to avoid glass shattering in the case of a bombardment.

Luckily, I have a bathroom big enough for a table. I've dragged one in and set it up with a small computer so I can keep writing. The computer itself had been left in Zagreb by a team of scientists working on the Distributed Language Translation Project, a new model of machine translation that used Esperanto as an intermediary language, which they had come to present in honor of the language's hundredth anniversary. The project required more powerful technology to develop further, so when they left the country the team no longer felt like lugging their old computers with them. I discovered one of the unused devices in the storage room at the office and asked if I could borrow one and practice my typing at home. Thus a DLT machine ended up in my apartment and came to accompany me throughout the war.

When I put the computer in the middle of my bathroom, I noticed the name of its former owner, Toon Witkam, on one of the cords. It was quite the strong sensation to encounter the name of the inventor of this Esperanto machine translator again and again every time the air raid sirens stopped and I got back to my apartment. I took the cord in my hand. Here was a little piece of the Europe that was trying to solve its language problems, while one of its peoples sent another its planes loaded heavy with bombs. The general who orders the shooting, the pilot that carries the bomb, the victim on the ground at whom the bombs are directed—there are no language barriers between them. What was Toon Witkam doing after he wrapped up his project while I set up his onetime possession in my windowless bathroom? What was Europe doing? The fighting in the Balkans didn't bother them or their comfortable lives. Europe wouldn't let it disrupt the flow of everyday events. To them, our bloody conflicts were as unreal and distant as a videogame.

On the windows, I had hung a set of curtains from Sweden, made from dark blue fabric and decorated with a flock of white swallows. A ray of light snaked its way into my room through one of the birds.

"Lights out!" yelled a frightened neighbor. "Third floor—lights out!"

That was me on the third floor.

That damnable Swedish craftsman could never have imagined that his curtains would take part in the new Balkan war.

In the morning, before the inevitable scream of the air raid sirens, I threw my swallows an encouraging glance. "Don't worry. This too shall pass."

These were, after all, delicate little birds from far-off peaceful Sweden that had been tossed into our chaos. Surely they must be suffering from culture shock. And yet, it appeared that the swallows had themselves transformed into warplanes.

The swallows were adapting.

I have decided to survive this war. That's all I have hope for. The silent prayer that my pacifism might also survive seems, at night, a very selfish thought. I am gripped by a guilty feeling like those Croats who live abroad and can do nothing but send packages from time to time with medical supplies.

In a country that has taken up arms in self-defense, pacifism does not sound right. Here, where everyone wants a rifle to protect themselves, the thought that guns do not solve problems sounds like treason.

I received a message from the international group Movement Without A Name capped with the slogan *A Man With A Gun Is Less Than A Man.* "Not bad," commented the editor of the paper, where I headed a section for early childhood educators. "But that won't work in Croatia."

Everyone around me has learned to distinguish between war and war *for Croatia*. This was a war for our *homeland*, they would say. It was a battle for the idea of justice. A cruel war, more hellish than those other wars finished long ago. Because this war was still ongoing.

The first victims were churches and hospitals, maternity wards and apartment blocks. The signs that marked buildings as protected works of art lost all meaning, transformed by these savage and lawless times into bullseyes. The symbolic red cross on the hospitals and ambulances was ignored. Croatia in the midst of destruction. Children and the elderly disappeared in the dust and rubble of razed buildings. Death reigned everywhere. Death became as commonplace as a sparrow's birdsong.

If only the bullets would come from some far-away people, but these bullets come from our closest relatives. We speak a language close to theirs. Our dearest friends live across their borders. I studied from their books and lined up their Cyrillic script next to my Latin letters on the shelves.

Today, librarians separate Serbian and Croatian writers, building a border station of hate between them. When a friend borrows a book printed in Cyrillic from my own library, he'll take it quickly, stealthily and guiltily turning its title page. He won't read it on the tram. Why provoke the others? The hatred of the shooter has seeped into the books.

I stood before my library, its books written in and inspired by Esperanto, by its green star, by "the world's only flag unstained by human blood". There I searched for inspiration and encouragement. The books stood silent.

Around me, in this world of people who do not how to defend themselves other than with firearms, my disgust for hatred invites suspicion. Am I enough of a patriot? How long will I tolerate Cyrillic? I, who believe that weapons cannot make the world a better place.

CPSIA information can be obtained
at www.ICGtesting.com
Printed in the USA
LVOW03s1930050817
543777LV00001B/1/P